THE BRAIN SINNER

By
ALAN E. NOURSE

ARMCHAIR FICTION
PO Box 4369, Medford, Oregon 97504

The original text of this novel was first published by Love Romances Publishing Company

For more information about Armchair Books and products, visit our website at…

www.armchairfiction.com

Or email us at…

armchairfiction@yahoo.com

A FORERUNNER TO INVASION...

He was an alien from a distant world, whose race had hatched a sinister plan of interplanetary conquest. His purpose was a simple one: scout out the target planet for traces of psi-presence. The target planet—Earth!

But this would be no ordinary invasion. It would be an invasion whose primary weapon was the power of telepathy—and the telepathic power of these alien invaders was tremendous. Only minds of equal telepathic power had any chance against them. So when news of the alien's arrival became known, a network of Federal Security agents—including human "Psi-High" minds—gathered to devise a defense against the impending alien threat. Unfortunately, the paranoia of their own people was nearly as great a threat as the aliens themselves!

FOR A COMPLETE SECOND NOVEL, TURN TO PAGE 79

CAST OF CHARACTERS

BOB ROBERTS

As chief of Security, it was his job to capture the alien—a hard thing to do so when government VIPs were working against him.

PAUL FAIRCLOTH

He was one of the best men at the Federal Security Commission, and loyal to the core—but what dread secret was he hiding?

JEAN SANDERS

She was beautiful, smart, and very telepathic—and she was also the bait in a desperate alien manhunt.

BEN TOWNE

Some said this cripple was the greatest man in North America, but others said that he was the most dangerous man alive.

THE ALIEN

His mission was simple—use his telepathic powers to obtain information crucial to his planet's invasion of Earth.

TED MARINO

As a PSI-High, his telepathic powers were needed in capturing the alien. Too bad he was loathed by so many of his own people.

JACOB BETTENDORF

He was a simple farmer from Iowa—perhaps too simple for the mind of a fully telepathic alien.

CHAPTER ONE

THE ship skimmed down like a shadow from the outer atmosphere and settled gently and silently in the tangled underbrush of the hill that overlooked the bend in the broad river. There was a hiss of scorched leaves, and the piping of a small, trapped animal. Then there was silence.

Higher up, the sunlight was bright over the horizon; here the shadows had lengthened and it was quite dark. Far across the hills a dog howled mournfully; night birds made small rustling sounds through the scrub and underbrush. The alien waited, tensely, listening, waiting with his mind open for any flicker of surprise or wonder, waiting for a whisper of fear or recognition to slip into his mind from the dark hills around the ship. He waited and waited.

Then he gave a satisfied grunt. Foolish of him to worry. All possible care had been taken to avoid any kind of alarm. He had landed unseen from Io.

The alien stretched back against the couch, allowing his long, tight muscles to relax, as he sent inquiring feelers of thought out from the ship, probing gently and tentatively, for signs of the psi-presence. The landing, after all, had been assumed. Already the natives had convinced themselves that ships such as his were a delusion. Such simple creatures, to disregard the evidence of their own senses! There should be no problem here when the invasion began, with the preliminary studies already completed, the disguising techniques almost perfected. A primitive world, indeed, but a world with psi-presence already developing—a possible flaw in the forthcoming silent conquest.

For psi-presence could detect other psi-presence, always, anywhere, despite any disguise. The alien knew that. It was the one universal denominator in all the centuries of conquest and enslavement in his people's history. Before they could come, they must know the strength of the psi-presence on this world.

The alien moved, finally, beginning his preparations. In the center of the cabin an image flickered, swarming flecks of light and shadow that filled out a three-dimensional form, complete and detailed. The alien sat back and studied it through hooded yellow eyes—carefully, oh so carefully, for there must be no mistake, not here, not now. The scouts had come and gone, bringing back the data and specimens of the man-things necessary for a satisfactory disguise. Now the alien stared at the image, regarding the bone structure and muscle contour critically. Then, slowly, he began work with the plastiflesh, modeling the sharp angles of his members into neat curves, skillfully laying folds of skin, molding muscle bulges and jointed fingers, always studying the strange, clumsy image that flickered before him.

It was the image of a man. That was what they called themselves. There were many of them, and somewhere among them there was psi-presence, feeble and underdeveloped, but there somewhere. He eyed the image again, and pressed a stud on the control panel, and another image met his eyes, an electronic reflection of himself. He studied it, and carefully superimposed the two, adding contour here and there, yellow eyes seeking out imperfections as he worked.

There must be no mistake. Failure would mean disgrace and death, horrible, writhing death by dissociation and burning, neuron by neuron. He knew. He had officiated at executions before—delightful experiences, but not to be trifled with. He stared at the image again and then at himself.

THE skin tone was wrong. The yellow came through too clearly in places, and, in this strange culture that color was reported to carry unpleasant connotations. He worked pale, sickly-pink stuff into his soft, wrinkle-free skin, then molded out the cheeks and forehead. Hair would be a problem, of course, but then there would be many small imperfections. He smiled grimly to himself. There were other ways of masking imperfections!

At last he was satisfied. There was no way to bring the normal reddish color into the pale green lips; there was no way to satisfactorily prepare the myriad wrinkles and creases that crossed the skin of the man-things, but with a little skillful application of projection techniques it did not matter.

The alien struggled into the tight, restricting clothes that lay in a bundle, carefully folded and pressed, at his feet. The hard, board-like shoes cut at his ankles, and the hairy stuff of the red-and-white checked shirt made him writhe in discomfort, but once outside the ship he was glad for the warmth. He stepped out onto the ground and listened again carefully. Then he made certain arrangements with wires, and threw a switch on a small black case near the air lock, and began marching down the hill away from the ship.

He would no longer need the ship. Not now.

The underbrush grew thicker, and he fought his way through the scrub until he reached a roadway. It was not paved. A flicker of sour amusement swept through the alien's mind. They had been afraid that these simple creatures might try to oppose them! Yet the scouts had said that far to the East were great stone and steel cities—the places-of-madness, the scout had said. Perhaps. But here there was no stone and steel, only dust, and the ruts of wagon wheels, and a howling dog somewhere over the hill.

The alien trudged on for almost an hour, trying to acclimate his legs to the fierce tug of gravity that pulled at him. And then he stopped short and listened.

He heard them then, in the depths of his mind, somewhere on the other side of the hill. His eyes narrowed. No psi-presence there, but two of the man-things, beyond doubt. Other whispers, too dull, stupid, vagrant whispers flickering through his mind. Lower life forms, no doubt. Possibly a farm with work animals. The scouts had said there were such. He turned off the road and almost cried out when the sharp barbs of a fence cut through his tender skin.

A trickle of green dripped down his arm, until he rubbed a poultice across it, and it became smooth and sickly-pink again. With a vicious jerk he pulled the fence out, post and all, and left it on the ground, moving through the woods toward the sounds he had heard.

Soon the woods ended and he saw the dwelling across a long, broad clearing. Black dirt lay open in the moonlight. He started across. There was light inside the dwelling, and the dull, babbling flow of uncontrolled man-thought struck his mind like a vapor. There were other buildings, too, dark buildings, and one tall one that had a spoked wheel on top, and creaked and rustled in the darkness.

He had almost reached the dwelling when a small, four-legged creature jumped up in the darkness, crying out at him in a horrible discordant barrage. The creature came running swiftly, and the alien's mind caught the sharp whine of sudden fear and hate emanating from the thing. It stopped before him, baring its fangs and snarling.

The alien lashed his foot out savagely; it crunched into flesh and bone, and the creature lay flopping helplessly, spurting dark wet stuff, its cry cut off in mid-yelp. The alien stepped onto the porch as the door opened suddenly, framing a tall, thin man-thing in a box of yellow light. "Brownie?" he called. "Come here, Brownie! What's the matter...?" His words trailed off when he saw the alien. "Who are you?"

"A traveler," said the alien, his voice grating harshly in the darkness. "I need lodging and food—"

The farmer's eyes narrowed suspiciously as he peered from the doorway. "Come closer, let me get a look at you," he said.

The alien stepped closer, concentrating all his psi-faculties on the farmer's mind, blurring his perception of the minute imperfections of his disguise. It required all his power; he had none left to probe the farmer's mind, and he waited, trembling. That could come later.

The farmer blinked, and nodded, finally. "All right," he said. "We've got some food on the stove. Come on in."

CHAPTER TWO

SENATORIAL Councilman Benjamin Towne slammed his cane down on the floor with a snarl, and eased himself back down in his seat, staring angrily around the small Federal Security Commission anteroom. The American Council attaché standing near the door retrieved the cane, handing it to the Councilman with a polite murmur. Instantly he regretted his action when Towne began slapping the cane against his palm, shod staccato slaps that rang out ominously in the small room.

The Councilman was not in the habit of waiting. He did not like it in the least, and made no effort to conceal his feelings. His little green cat eyes roved around the room in sharp disapproval, resting momentarily on the neat autodesk, on the cool gray walls, on the vaguely disturbing watercolor on the wall—one of those sickening Psi-High experimentals that the snob critics all claimed to be so wonderful. The Councilman growled and blinked at the morning sunlight streaming through the muted glass panels of the northeast wall. Far below, the second morning rush hour traffic buzzed through the city with frantic nervousness.

The Councilman tapped his cane on the floor, glancing up at his attaché. "That Sanders girl," he snapped. "Give me her file again."

The Council attaché opened a large briefcase, and produced a thick bundle of papers in a manila folder. Towne took them and glanced through the papers, lighting one of his long, green-tipped cigarettes from a ruby-studded lighter. "How about Dr. Abrams? Was he questioned?"

The attaché nodded in embarrassment. "Nothing doing. He ran us in circles."

Towne's scowl deepened. "Did you give him the Treatment?"

"He just wasn't having any, sir. Said he'd answer to a Joint Council hearing, and nothing less."

"Stubborn old goat. He knows I've got nothing that will stand up in a Council hearing." Towne went back to the papers again, still tapping the floor with the cane. "*Damn* that Roberts!"

The attaché glanced down at Benjamin Towne with some curiosity. It was easy to see how the man drew such powerful support from his constituents. There was something overwhelming about his appearance—the heavy jaw and grim mouth line, the shock of sandy hair that fell over his forehead, the burning green eyes, the stout, well-muscled body. The *attaché's* eyes drifted down to the withered left leg and the grotesque twisted foot, and he looked away in embarrassment. What was so awe-inspiring about a crippled man who accumulated great power? Towne certainly had done that. Some said that Ben Towne was the most powerful man in North America. Some also said that he was the greatest man, but that was something quite different indeed. And some said that he was the most dangerous man alive. The *attaché* shivered. That was none of his business. If he went probing *that* line too far they'd be calling him Psi-High, and he liked his job too much to risk that.

The inner door opened and a tall man, with prematurely gray hair strode in, followed by a girl in her early twenties. "Sorry to keep you, Councilman," the man said. "No, no…don't get up. We can talk right here."

Towne had made no effort to rise. He glared at the man, and then his eyes drifted to the girl and widened angrily. "I said a *private* conference, Roberts. I don't want one of these damned brain-picking snakes in the same room with me."

The man nodded coolly to the girl. "Sit down, Jean. Councilman, this is Jean Sanders. If you're here about the Alien investigation, I want her to sit in."

Ben Towne slowly set the papers down on the floor. "Record this, Roger," he said to the attaché. His eyes turned to Roberts. "I understand he slipped out of your hands again yesterday," he said with vicious smoothness. "A pity."

Roberts reddened. "That's right. He slipped out clean."

"No pictures, no identifications, no nothing, eh?"

"I'm afraid not."

Towne's voice was deadly. "Mr. Roberts, an unidentified Alien creature has been at large in this country for three solid weeks, and your Federal Security teams haven't even gotten near him. I want to know why."

"I'd suggest that if you read our reports—"

"Damn you, man, I didn't come here for insolence!" Towne slammed the cane down with a clatter. "You're answerable to the Joint Senatorial Council of the North American States for every wretched thing you do, and I'm ready to bring charges of criminal negligence against you in this Alien investigation—"

"Criminal negligence!" Roberts jumped up, his eyes blazing. "My gawd, Councilman! We've thrown everything we have into this search. This creature has played us for fools every step of the way! We didn't even get a look at his ship. It blew up right in our faces! Do you realize what we're fighting here?"

"I realize quite well," said Towne, frostily. "You're fighting an Alien who has slipped into our population, somehow, and just vanished. There's no way to tell what he wants or what he's doing. The potential danger of his presence is staggering. And you've fumbled and groaned for three weeks without even turning up a hot trail. You haven't even a coherent description of him—"

"We're fighting a telepath," Roberts said softly. "An Alien with telepathic powers like nothing we've ever dreamed of. That's what we're fighting. And we're losing, too."

The girl across the room stirred uneasily. Ben Towne's green eyes shot over to her viciously. "And you're using freaks like her to help him hide, I suppose."

"Jean Sanders is not a freak." Robert's voice grated in the still air of the room. "She's Psi-High, and she's the most valuable asset we've got in this search at the present moment. It's a real pity there aren't more Psi-Highs that have had her training."

"And you sit there and tell me you'd dare use Psi-Highs in an investigation as critical as this?"

Roberts sighed in disgust. "Councilman, you don't have any idea what you're saying."

"I beg to differ," Towne's eyes flashed. "I happen to be aware that there are a group of individuals wandering around loose who will have this country in chains in a hundred years if they're allowed to develop as they please. Psi-Highs are a vicious menace, nothing more nor less. We can't help it that we have them. The fools in the government were blind two hundred years ago when they first started appearing, and psi-factors are gene-controlled. But they can't use their extra-sensory powers without training."

He picked up the cane and leaned forward at Roberts. "Thanks to Reuben Abram's meddling over at the Hoffman Center, some of them are already developing their psi-faculties, learning to use a treacherous power that has no place in civilized society. Well, *I don't want them working in Security!* Is that clear enough?"

Roberts sighed tiredly and leaned back in his chair. "You're confused a little," he said. This is not the Rotary Club. It's not a Federal Isolationist rally, and it's not the Senate floor, either. It's just me you re talking to. And to my knowledge, you haven't succeeded as yet in removing all Psi-High rights. You've gotten laws through Congress to make them take tests and submit to registration; you've passed laws to prevent them from marrying; you've blocked their education and hamstrung their training and development, but you *haven't,* as yet, been able to strip them of their citizenship—"

"Not as yet," said Ben Towne.

"And you can't, as yet, dictate the activities of the Federal Security Commission."

"Not as yet."

Roberts' eyes blazed. "All right. Now you can listen to me for a minute, Councilman, recording or no recording. We've got an enemy in our midst—an Alien we've never even seen. We can thank a psi-positive citizen out in Des Moines for spotting him in the first place. He had the sense and the loyalty to report it to us. Normal psi-negative individuals can't see him, can't identify him, can't even get near him. We haven't tried Psi-High agents against him yet but we're going to have to, whether you like it or not. Psi-negatives are strapped. The Alien can run circles around them. Our only hope of catching him is to use psi-positive agents, the best trained we can get our hands on. Like Jean, here. And if you want to stop me you'll have to reorganize Federal Security to do it."

Towne lurched to his feet, his face white. "I may do that, Roberts." He reached for his cane. "I may just do that."

"You'll have to throw the Liberal Council out of office first. They're supporting me, and outvoting your American Council two to one."

Towne gave him a shrewd look. "Better start watching the telecasts, and newstapes," he said bluntly. "Already there are rumors going around about a mysterious Alien fugitive. Oh, I know it's top secret, but you know how news leaks." He gave a nasty smile. "People get nervous about rumors like that, especially when the Administration denies them so sharply. You'd better catch him pretty quick." He nodded to his attaché, and limped to the door. Then he glanced back over his shoulder. "Be sure to watch the telecasts," he said, and slammed the door behind him.

Jean Sanders stood up, white-faced and trembling. "What a vicious man," she murmured. "What did he mean, Bob?"

Robert Roberts shook his head, and fished a cigar from a desk drawer. "I'm not sure that I know," he said slowly.

CHAPTER THREE

PAUL FAIRCLOTH finished reading the teletape briefing just as the little jet plane slipped down toward the hangar slot in South Chicago. He slapped the spools into the erasure can and flipped the control switch to activate the distortion field inside the can. He stretched his legs, then, wondering vaguely whether he was going to come out of this whole mess alive.

Jean's parting hug was still warm in his memory, and he remembered the worry in her big gray eyes as she had kissed him and said, "Be careful, darling. I wish I could go, too. I couldn't bear to have anything happen—" It was the first time she had ever actually spoken that word to him, and he was glad she had. Almost defiantly glad. She had said it aloud, and she had said so much, much more without words. Only vague shadows in Faircloth's untrained mind, but he knew the meaning of those shadows.

A man was waiting down below on the platform for him. The hangar vault was dark and deserted. He took the agent's card and scanned it briefly. "Marino? I'm Paul Faircloth. Better give me a late briefing."

Marino nodded. He was small and wiry, with catlike movements and exceedingly bright eyes under his jet-black eyebrows. "We'd be wise to get on over while we talk," he said.

Faircloth nodded and stepped into the little tube-car that was waiting at the end of the platform. It was a tight fit for two men, and Paul ducked by reflex as it gave a lurch and dipped down the chute into a narrow tunnel, hanging free and speeding ahead on its electronic guide beam. "Is the Condor Building where he was spotted?"

Marino nodded. "In Center City, Chicago. First thirty-six floors are commercial, and the twenty above are residential. He's pinned pretty definitely on the forty-second, in a large residential suite. No idea why he chose it or how long he's been there—" He turned apologetic eyes to Faircloth. "I'm Psi-High—I guess you know. We've got him located and triangulated, and we can keep him pretty well pinned if he doesn't try to give us a shower. We're pretty sure he knows we're there."

"Shower?"

Marino nodded, grimly tapping his forehead. "A barrage, the works. This Alien's got a powerful psi. And I mean powerful. He gave it to one of our Psi-High men yesterday. It was savage. Nearly ripped him apart.

Faircloth shivered. "But you can keep track of him."

"Yes." Marino lit a cigarette with nervous fingers. "Roberts put Psi-Highs out to spot him, but he doesn't want any Psi-Highs in on the kill." His voice was flat with disappointment. "Political pressure, I guess. People couldn't bear to give a Psi-High credit for anything—" He glanced at Faircloth and reddened. "Sorry. No offense. It just slipped out." He bit his lip. "Anyway, that's what you're here for. Half a dozen other psi-negatives will help you. I hope God'll be helping you too."

Faircloth grinned tightly. "Got you nervous?"

"It's got me plenty nervous."

Faircloth nodded again, rubbing a hand across his eyes. "All right. I want your best men, every one of them, to go in with me. I don't care whether they're Psi-High or not. Neither does Roberts; he's with you folks all the way. But we've got to get this creature and get him cold. He's slick. Is the building sewed up?"

"Tight as a vacutainer."

"Good. Keep it under cover, and try to keep the Psi-Highs from broadcasting any more than necessary."

Marino gave him a queer look. "They'll do their best, of course."

"Right." Faircloth ran a hand through his brown hair and loosened his tie a trifle. "As soon as the building is cleared from rush hour, I want the power shut off all over the building. Elevators, lights, everything. We'll be on the 41st floor, and a squad will be on the 43rd. We'll close in together."

Marino shook his head. "I hope it works. They had him just as tight in Des Moines last week, and he slid right through." The man's eves were worried. "We just don't know what we're fighting. That's the whole trouble. Even the Psi-Highs are up a tree."

THE car gave a lurch and slid to a stop. They stepped out into a shiny tunnel filled with people emptying out of the huge building above. The two men waited to board an express surface elevator, and stepped off on the main concourse of the Condor Building. The last sunset rays made a dazzling golden display on the banks of heliomirrors, and Faircloth blinked, shielding his eyes a moment after the softer light below. Then he glanced at his watch. "Let's coffee up," he said. "We've got a few minutes."

They slid into an eating booth on the concourse and dropped in coins for coffee. It was so clumsy, Faircloth thought. Three and a half weeks since the ship had been spotted down along the Mississippi, and they were still just learning how clumsy they were. They had even thought that the visitor, whoever he was, had been killed in landing until the first Security Team had gotten to the ship. They'd gotten to within just ten feet of it when it had exploded. And even then they hadn't realized what they'd found, until the report came from Des Moines, and they started following up leads. They had followed the Alien, true, from the first farmhouse where he had stopped the night he landed, west through the farm country to Des Moines, then northeast to the great Chicago metropolis. But when it came to contacting the creature or capturing him—Faircloth shook his head. Clumsy just wasn't the right word.

He glanced at Marino, and then reached across the booth and buzzed for a newstape. He glanced over the Washington news hurriedly. Another upheaval in the Liberal Council. The Northern Democrats were trying to drum up Civil Rights Party and One World Party support for their new South American Development program, and they weren't getting to first base. And there was another vicious attack by Ben Towne on the Hoffman Center's training program for Psi-Highs. Towne had even named Reuben Abrams as a leader there, and worked in some high-grade anti-Semitic innuendo into the association. Paul went tense, searching for Jean's name. It was not mentioned. He took a deep breath. If that filthy dog ever dragged her name into public. He finished his coffee, and gave the repeat button a vicious jab.

Then his eye caught a small item with a Des Moines dateline, well hidden down at the bottom of the backside of the tape. He read it, frowning:

WOMAN CHARGES PSI-HIGH CONSPIRACY

Des Moines, Iowa, 27 June, 2157. A woman whose name was withheld today placed charges against Miss Martha Bishop, 23, of Oak Park Section, Chicago, whose name is listed in the Federal psi-positive registry. The charge was made at local Federal Security offices, and accused Miss Bishop of mental interference. The victim, who allegedly had information concerning the rumors of an Alien visitor, which have been persistently appearing lately, claimed that Miss Bishop had attempted to prevent her from reporting her information. After failing in this attempt, Miss Bishop was charged with using her psi-powers to erase the information from the woman's mind. Miss Bishop could not be reached for comment.

Mr. J. B. Dunlap, spokesman for the Liberal Senatorial Council in Washington, has

repeatedly denied that the rumor of alien visitors has any basis in fact. Nevertheless, the charges against Miss Bishop are being investigated fully—

Faircloth crumpled the tape with a snarl and returned to his coffee. Finally he nodded to Marino. "Drink up," he said, "and get in touch with your men. It's time to go."

Ted Marino left for the elevators to corral his men, arranging to meet Faircloth in the concourse five minutes later. Paul found a visiphone relay booth, and sank his long, lean body down in a relaxer facing the screen. The last of the rush-hour people were still drifting by in the corridor; Paul watched them anxiously. Then he gave a nervous laugh, forcing himself to relax for a moment. If only Jean were here! He battled an impulse to call her. Finally he dialed the priority code for the Federal Security Commission offices in Washington.

The relays clicked, and the code carried him through the front-line secretaries without any trouble. He gave a sigh of relief. He was in no mood to argue with secretaries. A moment later he was blinking at Roberts' tri-di image on the screen.

Roberts' face looked haggard. He nodded to Faircloth. "You got there, then. Good. How does it look, Paul?"

"Everything's just real nice," Faircloth growled. "They think they've got him pinned. The building here has a central power source, and we can bottleneck the whole place if we time it right."

"Don't miss, Paul." Roberts' voice was tense. "Whatever you do, don't miss."

"What's the matter?"

"Ben Towne has worked his way into this."

"Oh gawd!"

"Well, I can't help it, there was nothing I could do. He has the whole American Council behind him, and the Liberals can't hold out long on negative results. Towne has the whole picture now, and if we don't wrap it up fast, things here in the Capitol are going to blow sky high."

Faircloth scowled. "Did you see the newstapes tonight?"

"You mean the Bishop girl in Des Moines?" Roberts nodded unhappily. "Got the report from Des Moines on it this afternoon. Trumped up from beginning to end. I tell you, Towne is not playing around. I don't know how he plans to work things, but I'm afraid that story was just a starter. He'll do everything he can to tie the Alien up with the Psi-Highs in the public eye and you know what Ben Towne's like when he gets rolling. He'll play this rumor business up to the hilt. And the way things are in the Senate now, that could mean real trouble."

"Who's controlling Security news releases?"

Roberts gave a short laugh. "Take a guess. Just one guess. Don't miss tonight, my friend."

FAIRCLOTH nodded and signaled off. He sat swearing quietly to himself for another few moments. Then Marino came by, and he swung out into the hall again, glancing at his watch a couple of times. "Are you ready?"

Marino nodded. "Got the squads placed on the 41st and 43rd. Power goes off when we step off the elevator on the 41st. Okay?"

Faircloth grunted, and spread out a floor plan of the 42nd floor. "Is the building all clear?"

"All the commercial levels, yes. And autolocks go on all the doors but the one we want when the power goes off."

"Good. At least we shouldn't have residents underfoot. You've got Psi-Highs posted outside the building?"

"Yes, in 'copters. Circling the building fairly close, out of sight range of the 42nd."

"All right. We'll move in on him as soon as the power goes off. I want cameras going everywhere—in the corridors, in the stairwells, even in the 'copters outside. If there's a slip-up, I want to see where he goes, and especially I want a picture of him. A *good* picture of him. Maybe he can fuzz up human eyesight, but he'll have a hell of a time fuzzing up a camera. Let's go."

They stepped on the elevator, felt it rush up to the 41st floor. They stepped off. As the door closed behind them, the whirring motors died, and the lights went out. Faircloth led the way swiftly to the closed stairwell where they met four other men, one with a motion camera. "Cover everything," Paul said sharply. "If you see him, stop him with a shocker, not with pellets. We want him alive." He opened the stairwell and started up with the men behind him. Moments later they met part of the group from the 43rd; they started swiftly down the dark corridor toward the pinpointed residential suite.

And then, like a savage blow, a wall of fire exploded in Faircloth's brain. He gave a scream and jerked out his arms in an agonized convulsion. He fell forward on his face.

Wave after wave of searing agony burned through the inside of his brain; he jerked on the floor, trying to scream again, unable to force a sound through his twisted lips. He heard shouts around him, and a whistle shrilled; there were running feet. Somebody tripped over him, tumbled to the floor with a bone-jarring crash. Three shots rang out even as he dragged himself to his knees.

He was blinded; he had never felt such horrible, driving pain, and he clawed along the wall as more footsteps echoed frantically in the corridor. Suddenly Marino was shaking his arm, and together they burst through the open door of the suite as a roar of derisive laughter tore through his mind.

Faircloth opened his eyes and saw the empty room through a burning red haze of intense pain. He collapsed on a chair, exhausted, as Marino threw open all the doors. He gave a shout down the hall and others came running.

Unbelieving, Faircloth stared around him, then looked frantically at Marino. "You—you got him on the stairs?"

Marino shook his head miserably. "Nobody could see him. Not a soul."

The hoarse laughter grew louder in Faircloth's ears. "The cameras!" he gasped.

"Three of them are smashed. I don't know about the rest—"

"You're certain?"

Marino didn't answer. The answer was obvious. The Alien had slipped away like a ghost in the night.

CHAPTER FOUR

ROBERT ROBERTS was waiting, nervous as a cat, when Faircloth arrived at the Security office. There were deep circles under his pale gray eyes, and a dark stubble on his chin. He greeted Paul with a silent handshake; then they went back into the rear office, with its modern paneled wall looking out across the valley to the tall white buildings of the Capitol. Once it had been an inspiring sight to Faircloth. Now he hardly even noticed. A rocket rose in the morning air, leaving its white vapor trail like a pillar of cloud behind it. The weekly Venus rocket, probably, or maybe one of the dozens of speculator ships off for Titan. Faircloth scowled and sank into a relaxer with a sigh. "I'm sorry, Bob," he said. "It was a bust. I couldn't help it."

Roberts mixed a drink and shoved it across the desk to Paul; then he touched off the end of a long black cigar. "What's done is done," he said sourly. "You thought he was sewed up, and it turned out that he wasn't." He turned worried eyes to Faircloth. "What we've got to know is why he wasn't sewed up. Something went sour. What was it?"

Faircloth was silent for a long moment. Then he said, "I think the whole approach is sour."

"Very possibly. How do you mean?"

"I mean we're outclassed, that's what. This Alien is out of our league—way out. His eyes caught Roberts'. "He's a telepath, Bob, and I don't mean halfway. He's not just a feeble, groping, half-baked, half-trained, poorly developed Psi-High human. I mean we're dealing with telepathic power no human Psi-High ever even dreamed of."

Roberts' lips were tight. "Exactly what happened in Chicago?"

"That's just it, I don't know." Faircloth sprang to his feet, his face white. "Look, Bob, the building was virtually escape proof. The boys had every exit guarded three ways from Sunday. The power was off in the entire building, and there was no way he could get out short of walking through walls. And we had the walls guarded just in case he could. We got him sewed up, and then we went in to get him, and *Whammo!*" Faircloth clenched his fists, trembling. "I don't want to go through that again, Bob, not for anything. It was murderous. And the horrible part of it was that he wasn't using his full power on me. What I got was just a gentle rap on the knuckles—"

"And he slid through."

"Clean. Smashed the cameras; got away without leaving a trace."

Roberts shook his head, and fished a folder from his desk. "He didn't smash all the cameras." He shoved the pictures across to Paul. "See what you make of those."

Faircloth blinked at them. There were several frames, obviously printed from motion film. Pictures of a man-like figure running down a passageway. The face was not visible. "Not much help," said Faircloth. "Gives us a clothing description, maybe. Nothing else. He certainly looks human enough!"

Roberts nodded sourly. "At that distance anything would. Can't even get reliable measurements. And you didn't even see him?"

Faircloth shook his head. "Like I said, the whole approach is sour. You're never going to get him this way."

"You've got some ideas, I suppose?"

"I have."

"Well, I'm glad somebody has." Some of the tiredness left Roberts' face. "Let's have them."

Paul Faircloth lit a cigarette and slowly shook his head. "Sorry," he said. "First I want some answers. Straight answers about a certain individual."

Roberts' eyes narrowed. "You mean Ben Towne.

"That's right."

Roberts scowled and threw down his cigar. "All right, I'll tell you about Ben Towne. It isn't pretty. Frankly, this Chicago fiasco was the break Towne has been waiting for. There were Psi-Highs involved in that raid. Towne knows it. And he's going to build a story of Psi-High alliance with the Alien that will carry him to the White House.

Faircloth nodded grimly. "Does he have any conception of the dangerousness of this creature?"

ROBERTS snorted. "Of course he knows it! But Ben Towne is obsessed with a single idea, and it twists everything he thinks into horrible distortion." He leaned forward, staring at Paul. "Benjamin Towne wants to wipe psi-positive faculties off the face of the Earth. He hates Psi-Highs. Oh, I don't know the motives behind it. Maybe the fact of his own imperfect body makes him hate what he considers a sort of super-perfection appearing in the human race. It's a false premise, of course. The predisposition of certain people to high extra-sensory powers is neither a perfection nor an imperfection.

"It's just another tiny step in the evolutionary chain. It happens to be a dominant gene factor, and in our society it happens to put the Psi-High in a slightly advantageous position in comparison to psi-negatives."

Roberts threw up his hands. "But the motives don't really matter. Towne was smart enough to realize that there were lots of people who hated and feared the expansion of Psi-Highs in our society. He started fighting against it, and he's ridden that fight right into the Chairmanship of the American Senatorial Council. If he can split up the Liberal Council just a little bit, he can throw them out of office, and move his American Party right in."

"And where does the Alien fit in?"

Roberts shrugged. "It's obvious, isn't it? Towne has taken an issue and split the country wide open with it. And now, along comes a visitor from the stars, an Alien visitor who steps out of his ship and just disappears like a spirit into the population. An Alien who is fully telepathic. Towne can control the news releases; he has the power to decide on the security classification of information about the Alien. It's been kept top secret up 'til now. But Ben can control the news, and he can tie Psi-High humans and a vicious enemy Alien together so neatly in the public mind that every Psi-High in the country will be in danger of his life. It's political dynamite, and Towne is controlling the fuse."

Faircloth's face was white. "And if the Alien is caught?"

"All the better for Towne. Then the 'rumored' liaison between Psi-High humans and invaders from space can be 'proved.' Towne is in the driver's seat."

Faircloth nodded bitterly, and stood up, shaking the creases out of his trousers. His face was grim. As he reached for his hat, his hand was trembling. "That's just about the way I had it lined up, too," he said. "Goodbye, Bob. Have a nice hunt."

"Sit down, Paul."

"Sorry. I'm not working on Ben Towne's payroll."

"I think you are," Roberts snapped. His eyes flashed and he sat up straight behind the desk. "You're going to work with us, and you're going to follow through to the bitter end. You and Jean both."

Faircloth's eyes darkened. "Jean is not involved in this."

"I am afraid she is. Just as deep as you are. And you and Jean are going to do what I tell you in this investigation whether you happen to like it or not. That is, if you ever want to marry Jean—"

Faircloth whirled on Roberts, his eyes blazing. "What do you mean by that?" he said softly. "What are you trying to say?"

Roberts' eyes caught Paul's, and held them. "I'm saying that you happen to be a Psi-High, Paul. And I just happen to know it."

PAUL FAIRCLOTH sank down in the chair again, staring at Robert's face. There was silence in the room for a long time. Then Paul said, "That's a pretty bad joke, Bob."

Roberts nodded sharply, his eyes twinkling. "I'll say it's a joke. It's a colossal horselaugh on Ben Towne. He was so sure that that private file of his contained the names and histories of every psi-positive individual in the country! It's a horse on you, too. It's against Federal law to forge examination papers, Paul. It's against the law for a Psi-High to be unregistered. Both state and Federal registration are required. And it's against the law for two Psi-Highs to be married, regardless of their stage of development. Jean's work with Dr. Abrams has developed her powers amazingly in the last couple of years. Yours must be pretty crude, in order to keep them hidden so well—"

"You've gone out of your mind," said Faircloth flatly.

"Sorry, my friend. I'm afraid not."

"But you have no proof—"

"True, it's strictly a hunch, and a little personal investigation. You were through school when the registry law went through, and you must have found somebody to leak the examination to you early. How you did it, I neither know nor care. But all I need is a good strong suspicion to subpoena you over to the Hoffman Center for a test." He smiled at Faircloth. "Care to have me call Dr. Abrams? He's got some nice definitive tests—"

Faircloth's eyes fell. "That won't be necessary." He sighed, and sank wearily back into the relaxer. "I knew it would be spotted sooner or later. I even thought for a while that Marino had spotted it."

"He had."

Faircloth nodded listlessly. "All right. What do you want, Bob?"

Roberts' eyes were excited. "I want you to work with me. I think we can get this Alien and sink Ben Towne's raft at the same time. There's no single person in the country as dangerous to Towne right now as an unregistered and unrecognized Psi-High. And that's just what you are. And with you and Jean working this thing as a team, I think we can turn the capture of the Alien to the benefit of all Psi-Highs."

Faircloth nodded slowly. "It could be done if my ideas are any good. And they certainly would require Jean to put them across."

"Then you're with me?"

"Okay. You've got the aces." Faircloth gave a defeated grin. "I'll probably hate you for this but let's get Jean over here and do some planning. The first job on the docket is to pin this Alien and keep him pinned."

CHAPTER FIVE

JEAN SANDERS tossed her pencil down on the desk and flopped down cross-legged on the floor. "I think we're going around in circles," she said disgustedly. "Three separate circles," she added, with an owlish glance at Bob Roberts.

"All right, we're tired," the chief of Security sighed. "We've been at this for hours."

"It's here," Faircloth said stubbornly. "We've got all the information we need, if we can only pin down the application. Or at least we've got enough information to make a start."

"The more I see of the whole business," said the girl, "the more it looks fishy to me." She lit a cigarette thoughtfully. Her face was slender, with black brows and big gray eyes, and her slim figure made her look sixteen. "And it gets fishier and fishier the more we talk."

Paul nodded. "Exactly. There's something that we aren't seeing or realizing or that we just don't know about this creature."

"Well, let's try classifying what we do know," said Roberts. "We've got a picture that isn't worth a plugged nickel. We've got a few photos of the outside of the ship before it exploded. We know that he's psi-triple-high, fully telepathic, with the ability to fuzz up his observer's perception of him."

"Disguise," said Jean. "It isn't perfect. He needs that to hide the wrinkles in the disguise."

Faircloth walked across the room, staring at the walls. "Then there's the ship. It was found near Gutenberg, Iowa, on a bluff overlooking the Mississippi, three months ago. That's a fact. Farm kids found the ship but didn't go near it. Scared stiff. Told their father and he called Security. I don't suppose there was any way of telling how long the ship had been there?"

Roberts shook his head. "Biologists and geologists both had a whack at it, but the explosion destroyed all the flora and ground area within twenty feet of it."

"Well, anyway, no occupant of the ship was found, and no trace of where the occupant might have gone. Security sent a scout squad down to photograph the ship and it blew into a million pieces."

"That's right."

"How many of the million pieces were recovered?"

"About ten. Magnesium alloy. Told us nothing."

Faircloth nodded. "Okay. Then the Psi-High report came in from Des Moines, and you turned up the farmer and his wife who saw the Alien the first night. What was their name? Bettendorf, I think. Jacob Bettendorf. Rather dull folks. They fed him and sent him on his way. Noticed nothing odd, but the farmer said his eyes felt tired all the time the creature was there. How did their description jive with the others you've gotten?"

Roberts shrugged. "The same—or I should say, uniformly different. Nobody seems to agree. It's obvious that they don't actually see him in any detail at all. They just think they do."

"You know," said the girl, suddenly, "that's one of the things that bothers me. A lot of those people out there are Ben Towne's stoutest supporters. They don't like Psi-Highs. They keep their eyes open for people that act like Psi-Highs—you know, the way we're likely to nod and start answering a question before a person gets it half asked—or the way we sometimes forget our expressions when we've had an accidental peep at some sweet innocent young girl's inner thoughts. Those people can spot that. But the Alien went right through. Not even a suspicion."

"He got into the city fast, though," said Roberts. "City folks are likely to be a lot less observant than country people."

"All right," said Paul. "That fits well enough. Now, since he destroyed his ship, we can assume that he is planning to stay a while. That probably means that there have been others before him. He's too confident for an advance scout. He knew he could mingle, and stay, and observe, and learn, and get away with it. Probably his job is to accumulate information, detailed information about human beings, and with full-blown telepathy he must really be making hay. And unless I miss my guess, the information he wants most of all is information about Psi-Highs." Faircloth faced Roberts and the girl. "This is beginning to add up now. I don't think we're going to catch him in a dragnet. No matter how skillfully it's laid. No matter how many Psi-Highs we have on it, and no matter how well trained they are."

Roberts looked disgusted. "Then you're saying that we aren't going to get him, period."

"Oh, no. I think we can catch him. At least I've got an angle that's worth trying. We'll have no way of evaluating it first, because of the nature of the thing, but in the end we'll either have the Alien or we won't, and I think there's a good chance that we will. If we keep playing the Chicago game we'll lose every time."

"But what went wrong in Chicago?" Roberts cried.

"Nothing, except that we were licked before we started. Look at it this way. He's outguessed us every time. And if you analyze that a little, it's not really surprising that he has because he's telepathic. He does not need a twenty-page report and a road map to know what's going on around him. All he needs is a hint. Just a bare touch of man's mind, a slight flicker of contact, and he has enough of a head start to sit down and figure out everything that's going to happen from then on. Just like a chess game. You play along and suddenly your opponent makes a move that reveals a whole gambit that you hadn't been able to see before. But our Alien friend spots the gambit on the basis of the first move instead of the tenth. We make a move and he has it pinned. He knows we operate along fairly logical lines. He can follow out the logical possibilities before they happen, and there's no possible way we can trap him. Psi-Highs or no Psi-Highs."

Roberts scowled at him. "Then what do you purpose?"

Faircloth grinned. "It should be obvious by this tine. We feed the computer with all the evidence we have, and let it meditate a while and plot out a supremely logical approach to trap the creature on the basis of what we know of him now. Then we take that supremely logical approach, and change it a bit. We change it into a completely *illogical* approach."

THE call they were waiting for came through at three o'clock one morning, after they had almost given it up in despair.

It had been a long, heartbreaking wait. Time after time Faircloth had pleaded that they must have been very close in Chicago, closer than they realized, that the Alien was just temporarily frightened, because there had been no sign, no clue to the Alien's whereabouts, no sign that he was even in existence since the Chicago raid. Yet Faircloth felt sure that sooner or later the contact would come.

It was possible, of course, that the change in the search pattern had worried the Alien. Logically, a dragnet should have been set up in Chicago, and the entranceways to all the large cities guarded carefully. That was what the computer had said. "Probability is very strong that the Alien desires to remain in a city, but suggests that Chicago may not be the optimum location for him. Recommended heavy Security measures be taken in Chicago and surrounding cities of size. The probability is very high that the Alien is seeking some specific information. Advise close control of all spaceports, air, and rolling-road escapeways—"

And so forth. That was what the computer had said. Of course, the computer was far from infallible, but its analysis and recommendations were utterly logical on the basis of the information given it. That was exactly why they were carefully ignored.

It was a gamble, and no one was more aware of this than Faircloth. All Security personnel were withdrawn from the Chicago area, Psi-High and otherwise, except for a small crew headed by Ted Marino, who were scattered throughout the city. A gamble, but it was not entirely guesswork that made Paul so certain that the Alien, if left quite alone, would try to make contact with a Psi-High mind sooner or later. Of course, that conclusion itself was the result of logical reasoning. No matter what efforts were made to remove logic from the approach, it crept in. It had to creep in.

It was logical that a telepathically sensitive creature visiting a strange planet would seek to learn something about the segment of the population that could expose his presence. He would seek signs of his own kind of thought. Paul knew too well that a Psi-High mind that was cut off and alone was a sick mind. That was why Psi-Highs always settled in the cities, why they sought each other with such fierce, desperate clannishness, which in and of itself had bred suspicion of them in the minds of psi-negatives. It was not a matter of choice with them. It was a desperate need. And Paul knew how overpowering that need could be.

No, logically, the Alien would make contact with a human Psi-High, sooner or later. It would not be difficult to keep control of such a contact. The Psi-Highs were very few, numbering in the hundreds, scattered in colonies in the larger cities of the North American States. With painstaking care each one was contacted and warned, and those in Security Service were spotted in the most likely places for the contact they were waiting for. The roads were left free, and the airports and spaceports were not checked. An invisible network of human minds lay across the country, delicately tuned, waiting for the spark of contact.

Faircloth was asleep when the call finally came. He rolled groggily out of bed, his heart racing, and groped for the visiphone screen. Ted Marino's face materialized on the silvery curve; a frightened, shaking Marino whose eyes were wide with horror, whose hands jerked nervously as he unsuccessfully tried to control them. His voice was on the thin edge of hysteria. "He hit me, Paul. Just a little while ago."

Paul leaned forward, staring at the pale form in the screen. "Ted, are you hurt?"

"No, no. But oh gawd!"

"It couldn't have been just another Psi-High contacting you? It's deadly important, Ted—"

Marino shook his head vehemently. "No, no, no. It couldn't have been. I've been in Psi-High contact enough to know what it's like. This was different. It was like he'd lifted off my skull and scooped out my brains."

Faircloth lit a smoke, trembling. "Did you try to fight it?"

The man nodded. "I tried. He was clear in before I knew what had happened, but I tried. I—I think it puzzled him. It didn't do any good at all. He just brushed it aside."

"Ted," said Faircloth. "Now listen. Forget about it. Don't write up a report. Don't even think about it. As far as you're concerned, the job is over. Get dressed, and travel south—down to Florida, Rio, any old place, it doesn't matter where, just go. Use an expense account and have yourself the time of your life."

Marino's eyes opened in amazement. "Are you crazy? I thought this was what—"

"It is. Do what I say and don't worry about it. You're finished on this job. When you've gotten a good rest come back to the Hoffman Center and take up your training with Dr. Abrams where you left off." Paul flipped the switch and turned back to the room, his heart pounding a staccato cadence in his throat. He grinned triumphantly and began to pack his bag.

The chase was on, but this time, the mouse was chasing the cat.

CHAPTER SIX

AS IF a dam had broken, the reports began streaming in. Three more came from Chicago. Then a call came from Cleveland, from a Psi-High technician there who was not remotely connected with the Federal Security Commission. Then from Pittsburgh, then New Philadelphia. Like a fearful, ominous flood the reports of the Alien's contacts swarmed in. And Paul Faircloth and Jean Sanders were ready for them.

Their headquarters was a small suite of a room, in a middle class residential hotel in the heavily populated metropolitan area between Washington and Baltimore. Few of the Federal Security agents, Psi-High or otherwise, knew this. They knew only a visiphone priority code number, and a special word-key for scrambling. This was as Faircloth insisted. Of all the agents posted and assigned, only Paul, Jean, and Roberts knew the true nature of the operation, and each of them worked out their own illogical details without telling the others.

The wisdom of such a procedure was graphically illustrated a dozen times over for the Alien at work was thorough. An operative in Pittsburgh had attempted resistance to the Alien's telepathic overtures, as instructed, and suffered a burst of wrath that had left him blubbering in a corner for three days until a crew from Hoffman Center straightened him out with a week's diet of amphetamine and glucose. More and more, the Alien's puzzlement and frustration and wrath began to seep through, and Paul and Jean watched the reports, and nodded approvingly. Three times, when they were sure that the Alien had left a locality, they ordered cleanup squads to make raids on his former quarters, quizzing the inhabitants and neighbors, asking a multitude of idiotic questions, uncovering a half a dozen descriptions and leads that they assiduously ignored. Then they began stabbing erratically at locations where the Alien had *not* yet been, raids that were carried out with a viciousness and singleness of mind that left the unfortunates who were questioned quaking in their boots. On these raids, even the agents themselves were confused as to their purpose.

And there were other tactics, a myriad of disjointed, unconnected, abortive, harassing procedures, as though the whole search had suddenly fallen into the hands of a madman. A rocket ship bound for Venus was delayed four extra days in space, adding a half-million dollars to the cost of fuelling it. A whole series of roadblocks were thrown up between New York and New Philadelphia, virtually paralyzing the commercial traffic between the cities for two days. Quite suddenly, the order went out to close down on all passengers in the great St. Louis-New York rolling roads, and Robert Roberts put in a grueling week soothing the ruffled feelings of the businessmen who had been held up and the companies whose products had spoiled when the swift-moving strips had ground to a halt.

The news that there *was* an Alien from the stars at large, that Federal Security was waging a vast underground battle to capture him, was no longer a deep secret. The tension mounted daily.

And bit by bit, carefully sifted bits of information were dropped into the minds of the Psi-Highs who were still in the Alien's path. Long hours were spent in the headquarters suite planning the pattern to be used. But in the end it was a pattern well chosen and worth the effort because it was soon evident that the Alien was heading for the great metropolitan area that surrounded the nation's capitol.

No attempt was made to contact him. It had been entirely passive. The Alien's overtures had received no response other than futile attempts at shielding; no analyses of his contacts were attempted, and this knowledge was planted so that the Alien was sure to learn it. Warnings of traps were planted in his path, "secret" knowledge of closing dragnets and carefully devised Psi-High weapons to be used against him; occasionally such warnings were followed by abortive raids, either too early or too late to meet him, lead by psi-negative Security men who had no more idea what they were doing than the man in the moon. But one by one, key facts were planted, pointing always in one direction, aimed at one man, and always the Alien moved toward the city.

PAUL FAIRCLOTH and Jean Sanders seldom left their headquarters. Their job was to keep the pattern moving, and to plan out their individual parts quite separate from each other. It was terrifically wearing. As the tension mounted, both of them grew more haggard. Paul had not found time to shave in a week, and there were dark circles under the girl's eyes. Much of the time she just sat, tense, listening, waiting. Other times she helped him work as he fed data into the teletype and tape readers that had been set up in their quarters. But even amid the tension and exhaustion of the work neither of them could forget the simple, awful fact that Paul Faircloth had been exposed as a Psi-High, and that somehow, they would have to rearrange all that the future had held for them both.

Each morning they spread the reports out on the table before them. "Closer." Paul said one day. "And it's on his own volition. He hasn't been pushed. On the contrary, he's been left quite out in the cold. And he doesn't like it."

The girl nodded and glanced at the papers. "And he's definitely trying to ask questions. Karns' call last night showed that better than any other. And of course Karns didn't know any answers."

Faircloth nodded. "None of them know the answers. That's the beauty of it. Try as he will, he doesn't get anywhere."

"Not yet." The girl rose, walking across the room. "Paul, I'm afraid. We're shooting in the dark. We don't know what we're fighting against."

"Are you sorry you're in on it?"

"Oh, no!" She turned around, her face stricken. "I'd never want you to think that, never." His mind was suddenly filled with shadows, impressions struggling to get through, impressions that would make the use of words ridiculous. "Oh, Paul, I'm afraid! For you, for both of us. If anything should happen—"

"Nothing's going to happen, darling—"

"But what about *us?* If something goes wrong. Roberts knows about you."

Paul's eyes could not meet hers. "It was bound to be found out sometime. I'd rather Roberts knew than Ben Towne."

The girl's eyes were wide with fright. "But we shouldn't be together! Oh, Paul, how did he find out? Why did anyone have to find out?" And then she was sobbing in his arms, and he held her close, trying to comfort her as her body shook against his chest. "Jeannie," he murmured. "Please, darling, don't—"

"But it's so unfair! Why shouldn't I be allowed to marry you if I want to?"

"You know why, darling! It's the law. We tried to fight it but the people are afraid of us. There's nothing we can do about it. They passed the law, and they think it's right."

"Ben Towne thinks it's right!" she burst out scornfully. Her tears were hot on his cheek.

"Towne backed it to the hilt, I know. But people are afraid of a man carrying a single psi-positive gene, like you and me. What would they do if they doubled? How could we tell what our children would be like? Look, darling, think! You're just getting a grip on your faculties now. You're learning how to use your psi-powers, and look what you're doing! You can almost get through to me, and I've had no formal training at all. I've been underground, just training myself as best I could. You're nearly top-grade. Dr. Abrams says you'll have almost complete control in five years, and I could too, with the proper training. What would our children be like with the factor on both sides?"

"Well, what would be wrong with it?" The girl was fighting back the tears. "Are we such monsters? Have we done things so terrible that we have to be caged like animals and kept under control like criminals?"

Paul shook his head. "People only know what they hear. Ben Towne has been a terrible, vicious enemy, and enough people believe him to give him tremendous power. The people are nervous, and fearful, and there's nothing we can do about it." He pulled a handkerchief from his pocket and dabbed at her face with it. "We've got a job to do, Jeannie. It might be the most important thing that Psi-Highs have ever tried to do. We can't flop on this job."

"But Towne will just turn it against us—"

"Not if we work it right. And I've got a hunch that we're working it right."

CHAPTER SEVEN

THE visiphone buzzed shrilly that afternoon, and Roberts' worried face appeared in the screen. "Paul," he said sharply. "There are some bad rumors around. I think something's up."

Paul cursed. "What kind of rumors?"

"All kinds," said Roberts sourly. "They're saying the hunt for the Alien is a fraud, that nobody is doing anything at all about it. There were a couple of out-and-out charges that Psi-Highs are teaming up with the Alien to make an attack on the government—"

"Damn...can't somebody put the lid on that man?"

"That wasn't Towne's work. It was some other Federal Isolationist Senator on one of the propaganda programs that the Normal Supremacy party has on TV. There's talk that the Civil Rights bloc in the Liberal Council is getting ready to switch to the American Council side and force a presidential election. And that could put Towne in the White House. He's getting ready to move, Paul. We haven't got very long. The word has been sneaking out all over. Towne is behind it, of course, but he's smooth; oh, he's smooth. Congress hasn't been joined into two solid political parties for two hundred years, but they're doing it now, and it'll be a bloody battle. If Towne can get the Civil Rights bloc to switch to his Council he's got the Senate in the palm of his hand."

"Who's the leader of the Civil Rights men?" Faircloth's voice was sharp.

"That's just the thing. It has been Mike Veriday. His brother's a Psi-High. But his stock has taken an awful nosedive since this rumor campaign started. The polls have got him trailing Kingsley from Kentucky by three percent, losing ground fast. Now Kingsley, it seems, is in some mean financial trouble that Towne got him into, and Towne is ready to clear him of some nasty charges if he plays along—" He paused for a long moment. "We haven't got much time, Paul."

"Well, I hope we don't need much. But I think you can call in as many of our men as you need to. If things get too hot for you, list Jean and myself as missing, and throw out a dragnet for us. Because I think we'll be very much outside the law in another day or so."

Roberts blinked at him. "Better tell me what you're planning, Paul."

"Don't worry what I'm planning. The less you know about it the better. Just one thing, though. You remember Eagle Rock? The place we built up on Timagami when we were in college? Put three men at a number where I can reach them, and give them the location of Eagle Rock. Then tell them to stand by with a fast jet scooter. Got that? And don't let *this* leak, no matter what happens."

"I wish you'd tell me—"

"We're fighting for our lives, now, Bob. And for every Psi-High in the country. I won't tell you."

Roberts nodded, and doused his cigar. "Eagle Rock," he said. "You can count on it."

Paul flipped the set off and sank back to wait for the Alien to make contact.

HE STRUCK at ten o'clock that evening, with a ferocity beyond their wildest expectations.

They had known that he was near. The reports had come in, and they had plotted and calculated his pathway, and waited. It was only a matter of time, and the carefully planted information built a tangled, devious circle with a single Psi-High individual in the center.

Jean Sanders.

It had to be Jean. Paul hated it. He wished it could be him, that he could somehow protect her, but Jean Sanders was the only possible person to bait the trap. Her psi-powers had been developed carefully and painstakingly for years under the care of Dr. Reuben Abrams and his staff at the Hoffman Medical Center. A Psi-High individual was helpless to use his powers without training. Just as a child was trained through long, grueling years to use the mental faculties of thought, and perception, and logic, a psi-positive mind required training to control its powers of perception and physical control, if its powers were ever to be used.

Paul knew that all too well. He had the psi-positive factor, too. He had not realized, in his teens, when he had plagued and baited the two Psi-High boys in his high school class, that there might be a time factor in psi-positive development. Other Psi-Highs showed the signs of abnormal sensory apparatus at the age of one, or three, or seven. The schools caught them, tested them, registered them and sent them out into a life of fear and suspicion and hatred. They were considered freaks; the more dangerous because there was no physical identification that could be used to separate them from ordinary human beings.

And certain men had seen the great power that stood waiting for the man who took advantage of the people's fears. Ambition is blinding; certain men could see the danger to the comfortable, careless wielding of power if Psi-High minds were to work their way into government. But minds—like Paul Faircloth's minds—matured at different ages, and at different times. And some slipped through the barrage of testing, undetected, only to discover later that it was not the backs of the cards they were reading, but the mind of their opponent that held the cards.

The faculty was feeble in people like Paul. He could not read minds. He could not sort and integrate the confused tendrils of conscious and unconscious thought that broke like an endless stream from a human mind; he could not separate the reality of here-and-now thinking from the strands of fantasy, and memory, and supposition, and frustration, and desire, and half-understanding, and confusion that lay beneath the surface of those minds. He could detect falsehood and he could feel suspicion; he could sense love as he had never felt it before, and he could feel himself gripped in the helpless frustration of pity; he could savor excitement with a thousand tingling nerves, and he could sense the blackest depths of despair, but he could not sort them out to make a coherent picture of the thoughts streaming from a human mind. It took a lifetime of training of a Psi-High mind to do that.

But Jean Sanders could. That was why she was waiting in the room with him when the Alien struck.

She was walking across the room when it happened. She stiffened, screamed, and even Paul's untrained mind caught the impact of the wave of fear and revulsion that swept from her mind. She sank to the floor, and Paul stood by, watching helplessly as she twisted and writhed in the blind agony of the powerful invasion. "Please," she choked, white-faced. "Get me a pillow. Then—then listen—"

"Don't fight him," Paul whispered. "Let him in. Let him clear in. And then jump on him for all you're worth. Dig, dig deep—"

Her eyes became huge, like the eyes of an animal, frightened beyond hope, cornered, attacked and helpless to fight back. Her neck strained back and her teeth clenched. The blood drained from her face as she began moaning. "I can't, Paul—" she cried. "I—I can't get in—"

"You've got to—" Frantically Paul tried to thrust out with his mind, tried to dig through the wall of immense power that was present in the room. The Alien was close, very close, and the presence of his mind was overwhelming. Paul tried to break through, and then suddenly he felt a pang of intense white heat sear through his brain, driving him back, a sharp, savage stroke that doubled him up, clasping his hands helplessly to his ears as he fell and writhed on the floor in pain. And then suddenly it was gone as swiftly as it had come. He lay panting for a moment. Then he managed to crawl across the room to Jean. He sank his head to her chest, heard the slow, rhythmic pounding of her heart. He shook her, gently; her eyes flickered open, her face filled with horror and loathing. "Oh, Paul, I got—I got so little—"

"What did you get, darling?"

"Nothing. A picture or two, nothing more. Oh, he was so strong. I couldn't make a dent—"

"What pictures?"

She sat up, her breath coming in gasps. "Nothing definite. Ben Towne—yes, there was—something about him—just the flash of a mental picture, no rationality connected with it. And some papers, some sort of file I think—" She clasped her hands to her head. "He—he stripped me clean! I can't—"

"Jeannie! There must have been something else—"

She looked up at him, a strange light in her eyes. "I don't understand it," she whispered. "There was a picture of a farm—yes, a farm, and a dog, and blood on a pair of pants—"

Paul sat back, staring at her stupidly. And then, suddenly, a light flashed on in his mind, a flash so incredible that he hardly dared think of it. In an instant he was on his feet, the blood pounding in his throat. He began throwing clothes into a bag as the girl sat there, watching him dully, in growing alarm. "Stay here," he said. I'll call you—"

"Paul—where—"

"It's my show, now, darling. Wait, rest, you'll be all right. Rest, and say a prayer or two. Because I've got this Alien nailed for sure this time."

IT WAS incredibly dangerous and utterly necessary. Paul managed to find a visiphone booth in the rear of a station where there were only a few people, and quickly threw an adapter across the camera, and spun a roll of film in. The film started when the party at the other end flipped on the switch. The conversation was quite brief. Paul gave the street address of a roof-garden apartment in the Central Washington area, and then disconnected. After removing the film, he then reconnected with another number he had given Roberts several hours before. Ted Marino's face then appeared, and Paul heaved a deep sigh of relief. "How many men do you have, Ted?"

"Two."

"All Psi-High?"

"Certainly."

Paul nodded. "All right, we're beyond the law from now on, Ted. If you or any of the rest want out, take off."

Marino's dark eyes sparkled. "Roberts said this is the kill," he said.

"It's not the kill you think. But it's a kill, all right. Take the two men to this address." He gave the roof-garden number. "You'll need to have a jet scooter there, and make sure that nobody spots it. Use Security insignia. Send out a bleeper if anything goes wrong. I'll be there."

He rang off, and moments later was rising high above the city in his own scooter. In ten minutes he had reached the roof garden, and settled the little ship down gently on its gyros. He walked inside and sat down in the darkness, and waited.

He heard another jet scooter land. Marino walked in with two other men Paul remembered vaguely. He nodded to them, and they also sat down. Paul fingered the shocker in his pocket, his nerves screaming a thousand warnings in his ears.

The guard robot on the ground floor bleeped sharply. Paul reached for the lock-release switch, and heard the elevator start to whine. He unlocked the door and left it ajar, then motioned to one of the men. "Cover the hallway, and back them up when they come. Don't be surprised at who it is."

The man disappeared down the hallway. Paul sat quietly, and then heard the elevator open. There were footsteps, and a tapping sound. The footsteps stopped at the door.

"Come on in," he called sharply. "Bob'll be with you in just a minute."

The door swung slowly open and Senatorial Councilman Ben Towne walked into the room, followed by two tight-faced men. One of the men had a hand in his jacket pocket. Towne blinked at Faircloth, and his grin began to fade into alarm. "Who in the hell are you?"

"One of Roberts' men."

"Roberts said you had the Alien," Towne snarled. His green eyes peered around the room.

Marino swung on the man to the right, bringing him down with a stiff blow to the temple. Paul slapped Towne's cane to the floor, and pounced on the other guard like a cat. The Councilman staggered against the doorjamb, trying desperately to reach his cane. Moments later the guards were helpless, and Paul and Marino dragged Towne out to the middle of the room. "The files," Paul said sharply. "Where do you keep them?"

Towne's breath came heavily. "You damned snakes can't get away with this—"

"The files, Councilman."

His eyes went around the room fearfully. "The boys know where they are," he said finally, his voice so low it was hardly audible.

"Any duplicates?"

"Not of the files you want."

Paul nodded to the two men. "Take them down and get the files. Then turn the men and files over to Roberts. Tell him to see that the men forget all about this." He turned back to Towne. "You're taking a little ride."

"When this hits the papers it'll be the end of the road for you freaks," Towne snarled. "You can't stop it now—"

"We'll see," said Faircloth. "Now shut up and get moving."

They left the cane in the room. Paul helped Marino load him aboard the jet scooter. "Take him up to Eagle Rock. Keep him there. Dismantle the engine, if you have to—to keep him there. I'll be there in a few hours."

Marino nodded. "Should I report to Roberts?"

"Don't bother. Roberts would have a stroke. I brought Towne over here on a dummy visiphone film of Roberts, which will put him in enough hot water as it is."

"And where are you going?"

"I'm taking a plane west. I've got a visit to make. I've got to see a man about a dog."

CHAPTER EIGHT

THE farmer blinked across the table at him, red eyed and fearful. "I don't know what you want," he was saying. His voice was high and querulous. "I didn't ask no trouble of the Federal Men. They asked me all them questions, and I told them—"

"That's all right," said Faircloth. "We're just rechecking. You were the first party the Alien contacted as far as we can tell. The ship landed on your property, didn't it?"

The farmer nodded. "Over by the river. Scrub oak and elms standing over there on the bluff. Haven't never cleared it because it'd be too rocky to farm."

"All right, all right," said Faircloth sharply. "I want you to tell me what happened that night."

The farmer's eyes flitted to Faircloth's face and back down to the table. "I already told you twenty times. Why do you pick on me?" he whined. "I couldn't help that he happened to stop here. Heard him on the porch about ten o'clock at night—I was just gettin' ready for bed. And he said he was travelin' and wanted something to eat. We don't see strangers around here very often, Mister—" He looked up at Faircloth fearfully. "I—I looked at him, and he looked all right to me. My eyes were tired, like I said. I couldn't see him too well, but he came in, and ate, and I offered to bed him for the night. He said no, he had to make on for Des Moines."

Faircloth watched the man's eyes. "Details, Mr. Bettendorf. You've left some out along the line, haven't you? I have a report here that was filed by our field team that talked to you." He pulled out a sheaf of papers in the dim kitchen light. "Says something about your dog barking."

The farmer's face went white. "There anything wrong with that? I reckon the dog did bark. I don't remember."

"And you went to open the door, and the stranger was there, eh?"

The farmer nodded his head eagerly. "I told you everything—"

"And you brought him in and fed him and then sent him on his way?"

"That's right, that's what I done."

"You're a liar," said Faircloth. He eyed the man coldly. "Try the story over again. Once more now."

The farmer jolted to his feet, his eyes feverish. "I done just like I told you. I didn't tell no lie. I heard the dog yelping—"

"And you opened the door and there was a stranger there." Faircloth's voice was sharp. "Then what happened? Step by step. Minute by minute. I mean it, mister. I want the truth."

"I—I looked at him—"

"What light did you have?"

"This here same light. Not very much—"

"And what did he say?"

"He said, 'I'm a traveler and I'd like something to eat'."

"And what did his voice sound like?"

The farmer faltered. "It was funny—like gravel in a tin can. A funny kind of voice."

"And where was the dog all this time?"

The farmer blanched. "He—he done stayed outside. He saw it was all right."

""Where's the dog now?"

"I sold him. I mean he ran away. You can't keep a dog forever, Mister."

Faircloth's face was very near the old man's. "The stranger was out on the porch and you talked to him and let him come in. And then what did you do?"

"I—he sat down at the table, I think. I—I—"

"You went over to get some food from the stove, didn't you?"

"Yes, yes, that's right."

"And then you saw blood on his pants, didn't you? And you remembered hearing your dog give a yelp out in the yard, didn't you? The stranger had blood all over his pants and boots, didn't he?"

The farmer's eyes were wide with fear. He was shaking his head helplessly. "No—no—"

"And so you picked up your gun and you shot him, didn't you?"

And then the old man's face was in his hands, bending over the table, crying like a baby—huge, fearful sobs racking his bony shoulders. "He killed my dog," he choked between sobs. "He killed old Brownie, gave him a kick that split his head open. He didn't have to do that to poor old Brownie. I knew he was a bad one when he did that. I shot him. Yes, I did."

THE news broke to the nation that night, and the country went into a panic unequalled since the days of the Great Cold War. Paul Faircloth spent an hour on the visiphone from Des Moines talking to Robert Roberts, going over the whole business from beginning to end. The Security chief chain-smoked three cigars for the first time in his life. Finally Roberts put a line through to the Speaker of the Joint Senatorial Councils. Half an hour later, while Faircloth was making his way by jet back to Washington, Roberts was in top-secret conference with the Senate Council Leaders, and then with the President himself. And then the news broke. It was an official White House News conference, and it had been dismissed barely three minutes when the radios and TVs were carrying the casts of the announcement.

Faircloth brought his plane down at Eisenhower Field, and saw the crowd swarming across the landing strip before he got to the ground. A dozen flashbulbs popped, and before he could get into the Security Limousine waiting for him, he was in the middle of a tight circle of reporters.

"How long has the Alien been at large, Mr. Faircloth?" one of them asked.

"Sorry. The chief will have to answer that."

"Is there any doubt that he's telepathic?"

"No doubt whatsoever. I know that from personal experience. It's the only way he could move freely in the population."

"How was he first detected?"

Paul smiled to himself. "The President gave you that information, didn't he? A Psi-High citizen spotted him in Des Moines. The Psi-Highs have been on his trail ever since."

One of the reporters was tugging at his arm. "There's been a lot of talk about some kind of—well, liaison between the Alien invader and the Psi-Highs in this country."

Paul frowned. "If that were true, would we be working twenty-four hours a day to trap him? Use your head, man. There've been a lot of unfortunate rumors, I'm afraid. But I can speak for the Psi-Highs, and I think Commissioner Roberts will back me up on this—the Alien is menacing our very civilization. He's struck at one of our most beloved public servants in an attempt to undermine the government and prepare our planet for a full-scale invasion. There isn't a Psi-High citizen in the country who will rest until the monster is caught, and until Councilman Towne has been returned safely to Washington."

"But what about Towne's anti-Psi legislation? He's always hated Psi-Highs."

"Nonsense. Towne has been a loyal servant of the North American people. He's fought for what he thought was right, and has exposed himself to great dangers and personal vilification to do it. If he hasn't fully understood the Psi-Highs' side of things, that's not a matter for us to be vindictive about." He looked around the circle soberly. "The fact remains that he's in the hands of a dangerous enemy, and it's our job to save him if it can possibly be done." He nodded, and stepped into the Security limousine. It honked its way through the crowd, and then dipped down into the government tunnel that led to Capitol Hill and Central Washington.

He picked up a paper inside the car, and peered at it eagerly. The full-color picture of the President's grave face stared out at him in tri-di, and on either side pictures of Roberts and Towne. It was an old picture of Towne, a flattering picture. Paul grinned as he read the story rapidly:

COUNCILMAN TOWNE KIDNAPPED FROM SECRET MEETING

President Reveals Alien Telepath at Large

The President of the North American States revealed tonight in a special press conference that Councilman Benjamin Towne (Federal Isolationist, American Council) was kidnapped from a secret meeting with Federal Security agents last night in what was described as the first step in a plan for large-scale invasion of Earth by an Alien race from another planet. The President reported that one Alien, believed to be fully telepathic, has been at large in the country since his landing near Gutenberg, Iowa, last May 26th.

The Alien's presence was first detected by a loyal Psi-High citizen of Des Moines and was reported immediately to the Federal Security

Commission. Robert R. Roberts, Chief of the FSC, has been active in directing a nationwide dragnet to capture the Alien.

Councilman Towne left his home last night at 11:00 P.M. in response to a call ostensibly from Commissioner Roberts. It is believed that the call was forged by the use of a dummy-film, and the Councilman was reported missing when he did not return home. The two attaches who accompanied him apparently have suffered severely from the encounter with the Alien's telepathic powers, and were unable to be questioned at the Hoffman Medical Center this morning.

The President made special note of the excellent and selfless work of certain Psi-High citizens during the past months, in the course of a manhunt that has been shrouded in secrecy. The Alien's telepathic powers invariably overcame the efforts of psi-negative individuals, but through the efforts of the Psi-Highs, Commissioner Roberts has expressed every hope of ending the search within days and securing Councilman Towne's release.

Faircloth flipped the page, glancing at the smaller headlines. An interview with Dr. Abrams reporting the training program for Psi-Highs in progress at the Hoffman Center; a long article, discussing the value of Psi-High powers in combating a ruthless telepathic alien force; an article by Roberts, very carefully worded, explaining that if one telepathic Alien had come to Earth, others could be expected. Roberts expressed the opinion that human psi-positives were the nation's strongest safeguard against such an invasion.

Faircloth carefully folded the paper and spoke to the driver of the limousine. The huge car rose at the next tunnel exit, and sped north along the surface, then rose again. Paul waited, impatiently, and then stepped out of the car at the given address. Five minutes later he was holding Jean Sanders in his arms, while Robert Roberts sat chewing a cigar at the far side of the room, looking vastly pleased with himself.

CHAPTER NINE

"IT WAS handled beautifully," Faircloth was saying. "The timing was perfect, and there's no question but that it will go across." He looked up at Jean. "You're sure you got everything across to him when he contacted you again?"

She nodded. Her face was still pale. "He turned me inside out. Cleaned out everything I knew. I didn't resist. And then when we'd heard from you he contacted me again, and I knew that we were right. He's been in touch with me ever since. He'll be here soon."

Faircloth nodded to Roberts. "And you've arranged for the raids to start up through New England?"

Roberts nodded. He looked slightly high. "Everything's under control. Marino has a ship ready for takeoff, and we have guns up near Eagle Rock to blast it down. Ain't many people around in northern Ontario. The pictures will be rather bad, probably, but after all—field conditions, you know.

"It will certainly look like the same sort of ship that landed out in Iowa, and there won't be enough left when the blasting is over to tell for sure whether the mangled mess that they drag out of it later is man, alien, or oily rags. Those guns do a good job."

Something touched Faircloth's mind, lightly, like a quiet knock. He swung around, his eyes wide. "He's here," he said, and then he saw that Jean already knew. "Tell him to come up."

She nodded, and closed her eyes. Moments later they heard the footsteps on the stairs, hesitant footsteps. Then the door swung open. They stared at him for a moment, and then both men were wringing the man's hand, offering him a glass, and he sank down on the cot they had prepared for him, exhausted. "You must be dead," Paul said quietly.

"I am, I am," said the man. "Mind if I lie down?"

He was an ordinary looking man. He was slender, about thirty, and very pale. A single-factor Psi-High had no distinguishing physical characteristics; there really was no reason to expect a *double-factor* psi-positive to look any different. But somehow they had half expected a god-like creature, and he just looked like a frightened young man.

His face was mild and rather sad. But his eyes were clear and sharp, and the mouth was in a grim line, as he sank back on the couch. "I was afraid you'd never spot it," he said. "For a while it looked as though the whole thing would backfire. I mean when Towne was planning the shift in the Council and trying to force an election. I was afraid—and in the midst of that; you started your cat-and-mouse game—"

Faircloth nodded. "We had no choice. We didn't know, and you didn't dare reveal what you were doing at that point."

The man shook his head. "It was better this way, much better. I planned to kill Towne and then let you capture me. Counting on you to work the propaganda right. Then nobody would have known that the Alien was killed before he even got started."

Faircloth smiled. "The computer even listed that as a possibility. Low probability, but that was on the basis of what we knew. We hadn't even considered, it—yet every living Psi-High has known for a long time that someday two Psi-Highs would have a child." Faircloth looked the young man over. "We could only guess what the child might be like."

The man looked up at them sadly. "The child would be lonely beyond words," he said. "He would be able to hide, yes. He would be able to slow down his psi-powers in order to appear like an ordinary Psi-High. He could never have revealed it. Not even to his closest friends."

"And you knew that the real Alien had been killed?"

"Almost as soon as it happened. He died in agony. He had a powerful mind. He broadcast so wildly that every Psi-High within a hundred miles must have gotten a shower. I was in Des Moines, and got the whole picture clear as a bell. Went down and picked the details out of the farmer's brain. He was too frightened to tell what he had done, and nobody paid too much attention to him anyway." He shifted wearily on the cot. "The Alien must have been working so hard to maintain his disguise that the farmer caught him short. I knew it, and I knew what I had to do. I went ahead and did it."

"Of course Towne will fight," said Roberts later, when the man had drifted off into a deep sleep. "He's clever, and resourceful. When we 'rescue' him from Eagle Rock, he's going to know exactly what has happened."

Jean Sanders laughed happily. "I'd like to see him," she said. "I'd like to see him helpless just once."

Paul grinned. "You will. Things will be too far ahead of him by then. And of course, there will be a physical and mental examination. It will be a pity that the Alien left his mind in such a state of shock and delusion but maybe after a few months of psychiatric treatment we can find out the real reason why he hates Psi-Highs so much. And then, perhaps, we'll have a powerful fighter on our side instead of against us.

He looked around at the others, his face grave. "We can't afford to have the world against us again, not ever. *That* part of the news broadcast was perfectly true. There *was* an Alien. He *was* telepathic. And there will be others coming—maybe in a year, maybe in five, or ten, or a hundred—" He leaned back wearily in the relaxer. "We cashed in on it, this time, but we mustn't forget the parts that are true."

Jean smiled and put her arm around him. "They'll come, sometime—yes. But when they come they'll find the Earth well guarded." Her eyes drifted to the sleeping figure on the cot, and then came back to Paul's and held them. "When they do come, there'll be others—like him—to stop them."

THE END

If you've enjoyed this book, you will not want to miss these terrific titles...

ARMCHAIR SCI-FI & HORROR DOUBLE NOVELS, $12.95 each

D-61 **THE MAN WHO STOPPED AT NOTHING** by Paul W. Fairman
TEN FROM INFINITY by Ivar Jorgensen

D-62 **WORLDS WITHIN** by Rog Phillips
THE SLAVE by C.M. Kornbluth

D-63 **SECRET OF THE BLACK PLANET** by Milton Lesser
THE OUTCASTS OF SOLAR III by Emmett McDowell

D-64 **WEB OF THE WORLDS** by Harry Harrison and Katherine MacLean
RULE GOLDEN by Damon Knight

D-65 **TEN TO THE STARS** by Raymond Z. Gallun
THE CONQUERORS by David H. Keller, M. D.

D-66 **THE HORDE FROM INFINITY** by Dwight V. Swain
THE DAY THE EARTH FROZE by Gerald Hatch

D-67 **THE WAR OF THE WORLDS** by H. G. Wells
THE TIME MACHINE by H. G. Wells

D-68 **STARCOMBERS** by Edmond Hamilton
THE YEAR WHEN STARDUST FELL by Raymond F. Jones

D-69 **HOCUS-POCUS UNIVERSE** by Jack Williamson
QUEEN OF THE PANTHER WORLD by Berkeley Livingston

D-70 **BATTERING RAMS OF SPACE** by Don Wilcox
DOOMSDAY WING by George H. Smith

ARMCHAIR SCIENCE FICTION CLASSICS, $12.95 each

C-19 **EMPIRE OF JEGGA**
by David V. Reed

C-20 **THE TOMORROW PEOPLE**
by Judith Merril

C-21 **THE MAN FROM YESTERDAY**
by Howard Browne as by Lee Francis

C-22 **THE TIME TRADERS**
by Andre Norton

C-23 **ISLANDS OF SPACE**
by John W. Campbell

C-24 **THE GALAXY PRIMES**
by E. E. "Doc" Smith

If you've enjoyed this book, you will not want to miss these terrific titles…

ARMCHAIR SCI-FI & HORROR DOUBLE NOVELS, $12.95 each

D-71 **THE DEEP END** by Gregory Luce
TO WATCH BY NIGHT by Robert Moore Williams

D-72 **SWORDSMAN OF LOST TERRA** by Poul Anderson
PLANET OF GHOSTS by David V. Reed

D-73 **MOON OF BATTLE** by J. J. Allerton
THE MUTANT WEAPON by Murray Leinster

D-74 **OLD SPACEMEN NEVER DIE!** John Jakes
RETURN TO EARTH by Bryan Berry

D-75 **THE THING FROM UNDERNEATH** by Milton Lesser
OPERATION INTERSTELLAR by George O. Smith

D-76 **THE BURNING WORLD** by Algis Budrys
FOREVER IS TOO LONG by Chester S. Geier

D-77 **THE COSMIC JUNKMAN** by Rog Phillips
THE ULTIMATE WEAPON by John W. Campbell

D-78 **THE TIES OF EARTH** by James H. Schmitz
CUE FOR QUIET by Thomas L. Sherred

D-79 **SECRET OF THE MARTIANS** by Paul W. Fairman
THE VARIABLE MAN by Philip K. Dick

D-80 **THE GREEN GIRL** by Jack Williamson
THE ROBOT PERIL by Don Wilcox

ARMCHAIR SCIENCE FICTION CLASSICS, $12.95 each

C-25 **THE STAR KINGS**
by Edmond Hamilton

C-26 **NOT IN SOLITUDE**
by Kenneth Gantz

C-32 **PROMETHEUS II**
by S. J. Byrne

ARMCHAIR SCI-FI & HORROR GEMS SERIES, $12.95 each

G-7 **SCIENCE FICTION GEMS, Vol. Four**
Jack Sharkey and others

G-8 **HORROR GEMS, Vol. Four**
Seabury Quinn and others

If you've enjoyed this book, you will not want to miss these terrific titles…

ARMCHAIR SCI-FI & HORROR DOUBLE NOVELS, $12.95 each

D-81 **THE LAST PLEA** by Robert Bloch
THE STATUS CIVILIZATION by Robert Sheckley

D-82 **WOMAN FROM ANOTHER PLANET** by Frank Belknap Long
HOMECALLING by Judith Merril

D-83 **WHEN TWO WORLDS MEET** by Robert Moore Williams
THE MAN WHO HAD NO BRAINS by Jeff Sutton

D-84 **THE SPECTRE OF SUICIDE SWAMP** by E. K. Jarvis
IT'S MAGIC, YOU DOPE! by Jack Sharkey

D-85 **THE STARSHIP FROM SIRIUS** by Rog Phillips
FINAL WEAPON by Everett Cole

D-86 **TREASURE ON THUNDER MOON** by Edmond Hamilton
TRAIL OF THE ASTROGAR by Henry Haase

D-87 **THE VENUS ENIGMA** by Joe Gibson
THE WOMAN IN SKIN 13 by Paul W. Fairman

D-88 **THE MAD ROBOT** by William P. McGivern
THE RUNNING MAN by J. Holly Hunter

D-89 **VENGEANCE OF KYVOR** by Randall Garrett
AT THE EARTH'S CORE by Edgar Rice Burroughs

D-90 **DWELLERS OF THE DEEP** by Don Wilcox
NIGHT OF THE LONG KNIVES by Fritz Leiber

ARMCHAIR SCIENCE FICTION CLASSICS, $12.95 each

C-28 **THE MAN FROM TOMORROW**
by Stanton A. Coblentz

C-29 **THE GREEN MAN OF GRAYPEC**
by Festus Pragnell

C-30 **THE SHAVER MYSTERY, Book Four**
by Richard S. Shaver

ARMCHAIR MASTERS OF SCIENCE FICTION SERIES, $16.95 each

MS-7 **MASTERS OF SCIENCE FICTION AND FANTASY, Vol. Seven**
Lester del Rey, "The Band Played On" and other tales

MS-8 **MASTERS OF SCIENCE FICTION, Vol. Eight**
Milton Lesser, "'A' as in Android" and other tales

If you've enjoyed this book, you will not want to miss these terrific titles...

ARMCHAIR SCI-FI & HORROR DOUBLE NOVELS, $12.95 each

D-91 **THE TIME TRAP** by Henry Kuttner
THE LUNAR LICHEN by Hal Clement

D-92 **SARGASSO OF LOST STARSHIPS** by Poul Anderson
THE ICE QUEEN by Don Wilcox

D-93 **THE PRINCE OF SPACE** by Jack Williamson
POWER by Harl Vincent

D-94 **PLANET OF NO RETURN** by Howard Browne
THE ANNIHILATOR COMES by Ed Earl Repp

D-95 **THE SINISTER INVASION** by Edmond Hamilton
OPERATION TERROR by Murray Leinster

D-96 **TRANSIENT** by Ward Moore
THE WORLD-MOVER by George O. Smith

D-97 **FORTY DAYS HAS SEPTEMBER** by Milton Lesser
THE DEVIL'S PLANET by David Wright O'Brien

D-98 **THE CYBERENE** by Rog Phillips
BADGE OF INFAMY by Lester del Rey

D-99 **THE JUSTICE OF MARTIN BRAND** by Raymond A. Palmer
BRING BACK MY BRAIN by Dwight V. Swain

D-100 **WIDE-OPEN PLANET** by L. Sprague de Camp
AND THEN THE TOWN TOOK OFF by Richard Wilson

ARMCHAIR SCIENCE FICTION CLASSICS, $12.95 each

C-31 **THE GOLDEN GUARDSMEN**
by S. J. Byrne

C-32 **ONE AGAINST THE MOON**
by Donald A. Wollheim

C-33 **HIDDEN CITY**
by Chester S. Geier

ARMCHAIR SCI-FI & HORROR GEMS SERIES, $12.95 each

G-9 **SCIENCE FICTION GEMS, Vol. Five**
Clifford D. Simak and others

G-10 **HORROR GEMS, Vol. Five**
E. Hoffman Price and others

If you've enjoyed this book, you will not want to miss these terrific titles...

ARMCHAIR SCI-FI & HORROR DOUBLE NOVELS, $12.95 each

D-101 **THE CONQUEST OF THE PLANETS** by John W. Campbell
THE MAN WHO ANNEXED THE MOON by Bob Olsen

D-102 **WEAPON FROM THE STARS** by Rog Phillips
THE EARTH WAR by Mack Reynolds

D-103 **THE ALIEN INTELLIGENCE** by Jack Williamson
INTO THE FOURTH DIMENSION by Ray Cummings

D-104 **THE CRYSTAL PLANETOIDS** by Stanton A. Coblentz
SURVIVORS FROM 9,000 B. C. by Robert Moore Williams

D-105 **THE TIME PROJECTOR** by David H. Keller, M.D. and David Lasser
STRANGE COMPULSION by Philip Jose Farmer

D-106 **WHOM THE GODS WOULD SLAY** by Paul W. Fairman
MEN IN THE WALLS by William Tenn

D-107 **LOCKED WORLDS** by Edmond Hamilton
THE LAND THAT TIME FORGOT by Edgar Rice Burroughs

D-108 **STAY OUT OF SPACE** by Dwight V. Swain
REBELS OF THE RED PLANET by Charles L. Fontenay

D-109 **THE METAMORPHS** by S. J. Byrne
MICROCOSMIC BUCCANEERS by Harl Vincent

D-110 **YOU CAN'T ESCAPE FROM MARS** by E. K. Jarvis
THE MAN WITH FIVE LIVES by David V. Reed

ARMCHAIR SCIENCE FICTION CLASSICS, $12.95 each

C-34 **30 DAY WONDER**
by Richard Wilson

C-35 **G.O.G. 666**
by John Taine

C-36 **RALPH 124C 41+**
by Hugo Gernsback

ARMCHAIR SCI-FI & HORROR GEMS SERIES, $12.95 each

G-11 **SCIENCE FICTION GEMS, Vol. Six**
Edmond Hamilton and others

G-12 **HORROR GEMS, Vol. Six**
H. P. Lovecraft and others

If you've enjoyed this book, you will not want to miss these terrific titles...

ARMCHAIR SCI-FI & HORROR DOUBLE NOVELS, $12.95 each

D-111 **THE MOON ERA** by Jack Williamson
REVENGE OF THE ROBOTS by Howard Browne

D-112 **SON OF THE BLACK CHALICE** by Milton Lesser
SENTRY OF THE SKY by Evelyn E. Smith

D-113 **OUTPOST ON THE MOON** by Joslyn Maxwell
POTENTIAL ZERO by S. J. Byrne

D-114 **OUTPOST INFINITY** by Raymond F. Jones
THE WHITE INVADERS by Ray Cummings

D-115 **TIME TRAP** by Rog Phillips
THE COSMIC DESTROYER by Alexander Blade

D-116 **THE OTHER SIDE OF THE MOON** by Edmond Hamilton
SECRET INVASION by Walter Kubilius

D-117 **DANGER MOON** by Frederik Pohl
THE HIDDEN UNIVERSE by Ralph Milne Farley

D-118 **THE WAILING ASTEROID** by Murray Leinster
THE WORLD THAT COULDN'T BE by Clifford D. Simak

D-119 **THE WHISPERING GORILLA** by Don Wilcox
RETURN OF THE WHISPERING GORILLA by David V. Reed

D-120 **SPECIAL EFFECT** by J. F. Bone
WARLORD OF KOR by Terry Carr

ARMCHAIR SCIENCE FICTION CLASSICS, $12.95 each

C-37 **THE GREEN MAN RETURNS**
by Harold M. Sherman

C-38 **THE SHAVER MYSTERY, Book Five**
by Richard S, Shaver

C-39 **MARS CHILD**
by Cyril Judd

ARMCHAIR MASTERS OF SCIENCE FICTION SERIES, $16.95 each

MS-9 **MASTERS OF SCIENCE FICTION AND FANTASY, Vol. Nine**
Poul Anderson, "The Star Beast" and other tales

MS-10 **MASTERS OF SCIENCE FICTION, Vol. Ten**
Robert Moore Williams, "Time Tolls for Toro" and other tales

If you've enjoyed this book, you will not want to miss these terrific titles…

ARMCHAIR MYSTERY & SCIENCE FICTION CLASSICS
$12.95 each

C-40 **MODEL FOR MURDER**
by Stephen Marlowe

C-41 **PRELUDE TO MURDER**
by Sterling Noel

C-42 **DEAD WEIGHT**
by Frank Kane

C-43 **A DAME CALLED MURDER**
by Milton Ozaki

C-44 **THE GREATEST ADVENTURE**
by John Taine

C-45 **THE EXILE OF TIME**
by Ray Cummings

C-46 **STORM OVER WARLOCK**
by Andre Norton

C-47 **MAN OF MANY MINDS**
by E. Everett Evans

C-48 **THE GODS OF MARS**
by Edgar Rice Burroughs

C-49 **BRIGANDS OF THE MOON**
by Ray Cummings

C-50 **SPACE HOUNDS OF IPC**
by E. E. "Doc" Smith

C-51 **THE LANI PEOPLE**
by J. F. Bone

C-52 **THE MOON POOL**
by A. Merritt

C-53 **IN THE DAYS OF THE COMET**
by H. G. Wells

C-54 **TRIPLANETARY**
E. E. Doc Smith

If you've enjoyed this book, you will not want to miss these terrific titles...

ARMCHAIR SCI-FI & HORROR DOUBLE NOVELS, $12.95 each

D-121 **THE GENIUS BEASTS** by Frederik Pohl
THIS WORLD IS TABOO by Murray Leinster

D-122 **THE COSMIC LOOTERS** by Edmond Hamilton
WANDL THE INVADER by Ray Cummings

D-123 **ROBOT MEN OF BUBBLE CITY** by Rog Phillips
DRAGON ARMY by William Morrison

D-124 **LAND BEYOND THE LENS** by S. J. Byrne
DIPLOMAT-AT-ARMS by Keith Laumer

D-125 **VOYAGE OF THE ASTEROID, THE** by Laurence Manning
REVOLT OF THE OUTWORLDS by Milton Lesser

D-126 **OUTLAW IN THE SKY** by Chester S. Geier
LEGACY FROM MARS by Raymond Z. Gallun

D-127 **THE GREAT FLYING SAUCER INVASION** by Geoff St. Reynard
THE BIG TIME by Fritz Leiber

D-128 **MIRAGE FOR PLANET X** by Stanley Mullen
POLICE YOUR PLANET by Lester del Rey

D-129 **THE BRAIN SINNERS** by Alan E. Nourse
DEATH FROM THE SKIES by A. Hyatt Verrill

D-139 **CRY CHAOS** by Dwight V. Swain
THE DOOR THROUGH SPACE By Marion Zimmer Bradley

ARMCHAIR SCIENCE FICTION CLASSICS, $12.95 each

C-55 **UNDER THE TRIPLE SUNS**
by Stanton A. Coblentz

C-56 **STONE FROM THE GREEN STAR**
by Jack Williamson

C-57 **ALIEN MINDS**
by E. Everett Evans

ARMCHAIR MASTERS OF SCIENCE FICTION SERIES, $16.95 each

G-13 **SCIENCE FICTION GEMS, Vol. Seven**
Jack Vance and others

G-14 **HORROR GEMS, Vol. Seven**
Robert Bloch and others

FROM OUTER SPACE CAME THE RAIN OF DEATH...

Falling meteors are nothing new. Even heavy showers of these falling objects from the skies occur at certain stages of cosmic periodicity and can be predicted by scientists. But in this eye-opening tale, steady streams of meteors slam into the Earth, causing unprecedented amounts of worldwide destruction. Through all of the upheaval and loss of life caused by these deadly barrages, the scientists of the world searched for answers…could this be a natural phenomenon of some sort? Was the Earth simply moving through a massive field of space rubble? It seemed possible. But when it became apparent that the destruction was being targeted on populated areas—cities and towns—it soon became clear that Earth was not being subjected to a freakish occurrence of nature, but that she was being attacked—attacked by intelligences far beyond the comprehension of man.

CAST OF CHARACTERS

MERRITT

This brilliant archaeologist saw the first meteor strike—but at the time he never could have guessed its deadly significance.

HENDERSON

A man with far more knowledge than most of his scientific colleagues, he was soon to become the savior of the world!

FOTHERGILL

His wizardry in math and astronomy helped him figure out the real truth behind the deadly meteors that were destroying Earth.

BIXBY

This professor of mineralogy was ecstatic about excavating a huge meteorite, but it got him far more than he bargained for.

GILMORE

Just an average reporter looking to write a good article. What he got, though, was a story big enough to fill several volumes!

THE COLONEL

This red-faced officer wanted an answer to his question—could meteorites actually carry deadly diseases from outer space?

DEATH FROM THE SKIES

By
A. HYATT VERRILL

ARMCHAIR FICTION
PO Box 4369, Medford, Oregon 97504

The original text of this novel was first published by Experimenter Publishing Company

For more information about Armchair Books and products, visit our website at…

www.armchairfiction.com

Or email us at…

armchairfiction@yahoo.com

PROLOGUE

A SHORT time ago I was one of the guests at a dinner given by one of my London publishers in honor of my seventieth birthday. It was an excellent dinner served in the excellent English way, and over the cigars and Old Tawny, with the cheerful open fire casting a ruddy light upon the deeply cushioned chairs and high-ceilinged room in the Carlton Club, we became reminiscent. The conversation turned to anecdotes of famous men we had known.

"Let's see," remarked Gilmore of the *Illustrated London News*. "If I am not mistaken, you were well acquainted with Sir Paul Henderson, were you not?"

I nodded. "Yes, I was a very close friend—in fact, probably his closest friend. Why do you ask?"

"Because," he replied, "the fifteenth of next month is the anniversary of his death. We British revere him as perhaps the greatest of Americans. It occurred to me that as the only man living who *did* know him personally, you might be willing to contribute an article to the 'News'—something with some personal anecdotes, you know."

"I'd be glad to," I assured him, "but I doubt if I can write very much that is not already well known."

He smiled. "It's amazing," he said thoughtfully, "how soon a great man's personality, the details of the most important events, are forgotten. The man's deeds may live after him, the aftermath of the events may remain, but the details, the human side, the actualities, soon pass into oblivion. I'll wager ten bob to half a crown that not five out of the eleven men here have any clear, definite knowledge of Sir Paul's life and those critical years of 1932 to 1934."

"Nonsense!" I exclaimed. "Why that was barely forty years ago. I remember every detail as clearly as though it was last month. I'll take that bet, Gilmore, if you'll make it five quid."

"Righto!" he laughed. "It's a sure bet."

He won. But I should have known it. Forty years back doesn't seem long to one who has passed the seventieth milestone, but it seems much like ancient history to a man of fifty, and I doubt if any of the five had reached even that age.

For that matter, Gilmore safely could have offered odds and included eight out of the eleven present. Only he, Fawcett, and myself had much more than a very sketchy and cursory knowledge of those terrible two years, or of the man who, as Gilmore had boldly said, should rightfully be considered the greatest of all Americans.

In fact, my experience that evening aroused my interest, and I began to make some inquiries and investigations among some others whom I knew. The results were truly surprising. I found that very few persons knew any of the details or inside facts of the greatest crisis through which the civilized world has ever passed.

So, having supplied Gilmore with the article he solicited, I have put myself to the task—a very pleasant and easy one—of relating the true and complete story of Henderson and the Death from the Skies.

CHAPTER ONE
The Beginning

I WAS in Chile when the first meteor fell. I remember it most vividly. I was seated in front of my field tent in the Atacama Desert, where I was engaged in making excavations in a prehistoric burial mound. It was a few moments after midday, the sun blazed down from a cloudless sky, the vast desert scintillated, glared. Suddenly I was almost blinded by an intense green flash—a burst of light that I can compare only to that of a magnesium flash multiplied millions of times, a light so intense that the sunshine of an instant before seemed twilight by comparison. The desert turned a sickly, ghastly green, the blue sky appeared pale yellow. I caught a momentary glimpse of the sun, like a dull purple ball in the heavens, and then came a shattering, deafening explosion.

The concussion shook the earth, the chair upon which I sat rocked and pitched as if on the deck of a ship in a heavy sea. A puff, a rush of incredibly hot air, swept like a miniature tornado across the desert, my tent swayed, strained, and was ripped. Then silence, calm, the brilliant sunshine once more. Startled as I was, with my peons rushing madly from their quarters, screaming and praying, declaring the world was coming to an end, I realized instantly what had happened. Somewhere, not far distant, a gigantic meteor had struck. Falling aerolites were common enough in the desert of Atacama—though no one has ever been able to explain why they fall more frequently there than elsewhere; they lie scattered by hundreds upon the sand, and hardly a month had passed during my stay there but a descending meteor struck the Earth. Indeed, they were so abundant, their peculiarities were so well known, that the Atacama meteorites had practically no scientific value. All I had ever seen were small—the largest weighing only a few pounds. But this last meteor must have been enormous.

I could hardly guess how close to my camp it had fallen, but from the brilliancy of its light, from the rush of air following its passage, from the concussion of its explosion, I judged it must be very near. I was of course, curious to have a look at the thing.

Having at last calmed my men, I interrogated them, asking if any had seen it strike, if any had noted the direction in which it fell. Most of them had been far too terrified to take note of anything, but two of the more intelligent declared they had been facing the southeast, and had seen "the whole desert blaze into fire," as they put it, an instant before the report thundered in their ears. I determined to ride over and examine it in the cool of the late afternoon; and if it proved to be as large as I imagined, to radio to my friend, Professor Bixby, who was then in Santiago. He was, as everyone knows, one of the world's most eminent mineralogists and had specialized in meteorites.

But I had no need to send the message. Half an hour after the phenomenon had occurred, Professor Bixby was sending me a message. Brilliant light from a meteor had been seen in Santiago, had been reported from

Antofagasta, Tucuman, Iquique, Oruro and other points. Comparison of observations indicated that it had struck the Earth somewhere in the Atacama Desert. Could I give definite information?

I could and did, adding that I had intended to have a look at it that same day. But, as so often happens, plans go astray. That afternoon we uncovered a cluster of remarkable graves. I was fully occupied until dark, examining and carefully removing the contents of the tombs and the mummies, and the next day found me still busy with the find, which to me was far more interesting and important than all the meteorites that had ever fallen.

And, on the second day, another visitor dropped unexpectedly from the skies. This time it was a big military bombing plane, and from it stepped Professor Bixby and three assistants. He had lost no time in reaching the scene; he had come prepared to make an exhaustive investigation and study of the largest aerolite that had struck Earth in many years—centuries probably. He had already located it from the plane but explained that owing to the broken character of the surrounding desert near where the meteorite had fallen—about forty miles from my camp—a landing in its vicinity was impossible. Hence he had come to me as the nearest inhabitant of the desert. Of course I welcomed him, offered him the limited hospitality and resources of my camp as long as he wished to remain, and assured him he was welcome to the use of spare horses and pack-mules for transporting himself and his equipment to the meteorite, where he planned to remain for some time.

The plane, having disgorged its cargo, taxied across the desert sands, rose slowly and regretfully, like a vulture disturbed at a meal, circled and roared off towards Santiago. The next day Professor Bixby and his men and three of my peons took their departure and headed for the southeast.

I gave little thought to the Professor in the days that followed, but when a fortnight had passed and I had heard nothing from him, I began to feel troubled. He had carried water and provisions for ten days and had arranged to send back a peon for additional supplies before his stock was exhausted. But two weeks had gone and no peon had shown up. Very likely, I thought—laughing at my own fears—the supplies had lasted longer than he had expected; he had probably found that he would be through with his work in a few days, and he had decided he would not require more supplies for the short time remaining before he returned to join me.

Yet I could not help worrying. Bixby, I knew, was no amateur at desert work. He had made expeditions into the Gobi, the Sahara, the Arabian and our own western deserts. He was an old hand at field work, and yet when eighteen days had gone by I decided something *must* have gone wrong, and I forthwith set out to find him.

Not until we had ridden for miles did I realize what little chance there was. I had neglected to secure accurate details, and the exact bearings of the meteorite. The desert was vast; it was seamed with gullies, broken by ridges, and nowhere was it possible to see more than a short distance in any direction. And during the two weeks and more that had passed, the drifting sand had completely obliterated any trail that might have led us to Professor Bixby's camp. Baffled, I returned to my camp and at once sent a radio message to Santiago, reporting conditions and asking that a plane be sent in search of the Professor and his party.

The response was prompt. Soon after daybreak, the big bomber swept down as before. Anxious and troubled, I climbed in. A moment later we were off and rushing into the sunrise. It was the same pilot who had accompanied Professor Bixby before, and he knew very nearly where the meteorite lay.

He had no difficulty in locating it, but there was no sign of life, no moving figures in the vicinity. What had happened? Dropping down, he circled over the spot as low as he dared. I stared, could scarcely believe my eyes. My worst fears were realized. Stretched upon the sand, scarcely distinguishable from the rocks and surroundings as we circled over them, were the motionless bodies of men, horses, and mules! It was horrible—ghastly. As if in a nightmare, I counted them: three, five, six, seven men dead—corpses under the blazing sun! I was glad we could not land.

I shuddered to think of what we would find—of the horrors that would greet us now that the vultures had finished, for the loathsome black birds, like specks of coal upon the brown sand, were motionless, apparently gorged to repletion. Strange, I thought, that they did not move, did not flap their broad wings, showed no fright at our roaring motors and passing shadow! And then I gasped. Seizing the powerful glasses beside me, I focused them on the ghastly scene below. I was right. The vultures, too, were dead! There was not a living thing upon the desert beneath us! What did it mean? What had destroyed those ominous black birds? I was filled with a vague dread, a horror of the place, and I was more than ever thankful that it was impossible for us to land.

There seemed to be nothing that we could do except return to camp, travel across the desert and bury the bodies. But all other thoughts were temporarily driven from my mind by the news that awaited me at my camp. From various quarters of the world word had been flashed about the falling of huge meteors. Several had dropped in Brazil, others had struck upon the Argentine Pampas, one or two had been seen in our own Southwest. Terrified Bedouins had brought reports of blazing stars falling in the wastes of the Sahara; from far-off Greenland a wireless message had flashed news of a blinding flash, a terrific concussion in the bleak Arctic, and several vessels had radioed stories of witnessing the passage of huge meteors that seemed to drop into the sea.

Intently I perused the bundle of papers that had arrived with my mail from the mining camp at Chuquicamata during my absence. I studied the dates of the falling stars. They had not come all together. Several days—a week in fact—had elapsed between the time the meteorite fell so unpleasantly close to my camp and that which struck the Earth somewhere in Arizona. The others had come, sometimes two or three in one day, at other times at intervals of several days. Evidently Earth was passing through an area of outer space that was heavy with meteors, but unlike such showers in the past, all these appeared to be of unusual size, and their appearance had not been forecast by astronomers.

The papers were filled with fanciful conjectures as to what might happen if one of the huge masses should fall in a large city or in a crowd. Imagine the loss of life, wrote some scare-head reporter, if such a mass of white-hot metal, projected with greater force than if hurled from any cannon, should strike a huge ocean liner. Imagine the death and destruction it would cause should it sweep down upon Times Square, Piccadilly Circus, the Place de l'Opera or any other crowded section of a great capital. But no casualty *had* resulted. It was merely a remarkable, unprecedented phenomenon. Scarcely glancing at the matter-of-fact statements regarding scientific expeditions that were preparing to investigate and study the celestial visitors (for it appeared all had fortunately struck in remote uninhabited districts) I tossed aside the papers and got busy with my neglected work, mentally deciding to set out with my men to inter the bodies of Professor Bixby and his companions the next day. First, however, I wrote a report of the tragedy, addressed it to the American Minister at Santiago, and handing it to the waiting pilot, I then bade him farewell.

Scarcely had he vanished to the south when I received a radio message. It was from Griffin of the *West Coast Herald* at Antofagasta, asking information of Bixby and imparting more news. "Understand Bixby investigating meteor Atacama Desert," it ran. "Can you radio summary results? Report from Kenya. Cape to Cairo express train struck by meteor—completely destroyed. Incoming vessels report thousands of fish and whales dead, supposedly due to meteors. No word received from any other scientists."

The matter was getting serious. A meteorite had by chance struck where it had taken a toll of human lives. I radioed back: "Bixby and companions dead. Probably thirst. Recovering bodies tomorrow. Seen only from plane."

Yet, as I sat pondering on the matter, I could not understand how it was possible that the Professor and his men had all died of thirst. Why hadn't he sent to me for water and supplies? He must have realized that he was getting short. And even if by some accident the last of the water had been lost, he could have reached my camp. A day's riding would have done it, and he had horses and mules. The more I thought of it the more puzzled I became. Death by thirst doesn't come suddenly, doesn't strike down seven men at one time. And the horses and mules? They would have found their way to water or to my camp.

The first vague, unreasonable dread that had possessed me in the circling plane returned to me. The dead men, the dead animals, the dead vultures! It was as if they had been struck down, suddenly destroyed by some malignant, invisible thing. What could it have been? Could it have had any connection with the meteorite? Of course not, I decided. How could an aerolite affect men, at least after it had struck the Earth and had cooled? Impossible!

I was then interrupted by another message. This time it was from Santiago, from the American Embassy: "Report received. Regret to learn fate of Bixby. Advise when bodies recovered."

Nothing startling in that at any rate. But as I continued with my excavations, I began to have a most unaccountable distaste for visiting the vicinity of the meteorite and recovering the bodies. There was no reason for my feelings, no sense in them. I was not squeamish, not sentimental, not afraid, not superstitious regarding human cadavers. I, an ethnologist, had violated far too many graves, had disinterred far too many dead, had handled far too many bodies in all stages of preservation to have any squeamish ideas left regarding them. To me a corpse was no more than so much animal matter devoid of life—usually a specimen.

But that does not mean that I had no sentiment for Professor Bixby's remains, that I was callous. Although, as far as I was concerned, my own body—once life had left it—might remain to wither and dry upon a desert, or might sink to the depths of the sea, yet I realized and appreciated the fact that other persons did not feel the same; that Professor Bixby's friends and relatives would no doubt feel easier if his remains were, to use the accepted term, given Christian burial, and that it was my duty to attend to the matter.

Still, for some inexplicable reason, I tried to find an excuse for not doing so. It was a long, hard journey. I had a great deal to do. The bodies were safe there, why should I be in a hurry to attend to them? I would put the disagreeable duty off for a day or two. That night the second meteorite fell. I was awakened from a sound sleep by the fearful green glare. The ground seemed to spring up beneath my cot with the concussion of the explosion. I was thrown to the earth and half-stunned. I heard the terrified shouts and prayers of my men.

Where the thing struck I never knew, put that it was either nearer than the first, or was far larger, was obvious. I admit I was frightened. There was no more sleep for anyone that night, and at daybreak my peons delivered their ultimatum. The place was cursed, they declared. I had brought down the vengeance of the gods by digging up the dead; they were leaving the unholy spot right away. I cannot say I blamed them, even though it meant the end of my work, the practical failure of my expedition. And I could not remain there alone even if I had wanted to do so. There was nothing for me to do, but to pack up and go. The men would not even wait to attend to the burial of Professor Bixby and his dead comrades, and by mid-afternoon our pack train was winding its way across the desert towards Itchicama, the nearest railway station to the north.

CHAPTER TWO
One Chance in Millions

I FIRST learned of the developments that were taking place when after arriving at Antofagasta, I strolled into the Anglo-American Club and glanced over the files of newspapers. Every one bore screaming headlines regarding the barrage of meteors that was now exciting the entire world. Naturally, having been literally driven from my cherished work by a meteorite, I was intensely interested, but if I was to obtain any connected idea of what was taking and had taken place, it was essential that I begin at the beginning, or at least with what followed the news I had already seen. Presently I found it in the West Coast Herald of the 26th, "PROMINENT SCIENTIST SACRIFICES LIFE TO FIRST METEOR," I read. I glanced rapidly down the page. First there was my radio message to Griffin. I read on:

"The above message from Dr. Merritt, engaged in archeological work in the Atacama desert, is the first definite news received of Professor Bixby and his assistants who left Santiago nearly three weeks ago with the purpose of investigating the first of the giant meteors that have fallen. It will be remembered that Dr. Merritt first reported this meteor when he sent a radio message to Professor Bixby. Although the message quoted above implies that the scientist and his companions succumbed to thirst, it appears highly improbable to us. The party was within a day's ride of Dr. Merritt's camp—where abundant supplies were available—and it seems incredible that an entire party of seven men should have died for want of water under the circumstances. It seems far more reasonable to suppose that the unfortunate men were killed by bandits, who, having seen the meteor fall, hurried to it with the expectation of finding treasure, and finding Professor Bixby's party on the scene, murdered the men for the purpose of robbery. It is a common belief among the natives that meteorites frequently contain gold and diamonds, a belief due probably to the fact that in former years large sums were paid for meteorites by scientists and museums. Nothing can be definitely determined, however, until the bodies are recovered; for Dr. Merritt's discovery of the fate of the unfortunate men was made from an airplane, which, owing to the terrain, was unable to effect a landing in the vicinity.

"Reports of other meteorites having fallen in various parts of the world are still being received. Up to the present time, however, the only direct loss of life or property reported is that of the Cape to Cairo express near Kenya, a report that is still unconfirmed.

"The unprecedented fall of many meteors of unusual size has created a widespread interest, especially among scientists. No reports have yet been received from the several expeditions that have set out to investigate these strange celestial visitors."

I picked up the *Commercio* of the 21st. "METEOR CAUSES LOSS OF 300 LIVES NEAR KENYA," I read, in heavy black type across the top of the front page. Then, in smaller type: "Reports of Destruction of Life by Meteor on Cape to Cairo Express Confirmed. Astounding Story Comes From Africa."

And astounding it was. According to the official reports, the train had not been destroyed by a meteorite as first reported. A rescue and relief train sent out from Kenya had found the express derailed and partly wrecked where it had taken a sharp curve at terrific speed. There was no trace of a meteorite having struck it nor of an aerolite in the vicinity. But *every soul on the train, including the engineer and fireman, had been killed.* Strangest of all was the fact that few of the dead showed signs of having been injured when the train left the rails, and these, the surgeons declared, had been dead when the injuries were received. The only plausible theory was that the meteor had struck near the train and that the shock, or the blast of heated air, or possibly gases from the molten mass, had asphyxiated the occupants of the train, which had continued to speed on until it left the rails.

The story concluded with a report from Lima that pilots of the Peruvian Airways Company arriving from Iquitos had—while flying over the vast Amazonian forest—noticed extensive areas of dead and leveled trees, and that good-sized Indian villages in the vicinity had appeared deserted. It was assumed that these circular areas of destroyed jungle marked the descent of several huge meteors that had been reported from various points in Peru, Brazil, and Ecuador.

Evidently no new meteors had been seen for the next few days, for the papers reported none. Instead, they devoted their columns to speculations and the theories and the opinions of eminent scientists and astronomers on the subject. For once there appeared to be little dissent among scientific men. All agreed that the immense size of the meteorites was unprecedented, but declared that otherwise the shower had not been unusual or remarkable.

They pointed out that meteors fall almost nightly, that many reach Earth each year, and that many meteoric showers of much longer duration and of many more aerolites had repeatedly been witnessed and recorded in the past. Had the recent meteorites been of usual size the shower would have caused no comment.

Scientifically it was extremely interesting and very fortunate, for there would now be an adequate supply of meteoric material to enable a complete and exhaustive analysis and examination to be made. New elements and minerals might be discovered; the results might throw a new light upon the composition of the planets, stars, and comets. Indeed, the total mass of meteoric material might be sufficient to be of commercial value. Whether they were stony or metallic could not be stated as none of the expeditions had yet supported their findings. And they unanimously agreed that the danger to human life or to property—even if the fall continued—was almost negligible.

They pointed out that all the cities and settlements on the globe, if placed together, would cover only a very minute portion of Earth's surface; that scattered as they were, there was not one chance in millions of a meteorite striking a town, and they triumphantly pointed to the fact that, as far as known, no city had ever yet been destroyed by a falling meteorite during the world's history. The chances of human beings being struck were even smaller. There were only two records of such casualties known.

That hundreds of persons had been killed on the African express was indisputable. The only logical hypothesis to account for it was that the meteor had passed close to the train, that its tremendous heat had generated noxious gases that had destroyed the crew and passengers. But the scientists declared such a disaster might never happen again; it was mere chance—one chance in millions.

The effect of the unprecedented descent of the meteors upon the public as a whole was, however, quite different. Many people of a religious nature saw in the phenomena the approaching end of the world. Fanatical orators stood on street corners calling on the people to repent and prepare for death. They recalled the Biblical story of Sodom and Gomorrah. They exhorted, prayed, and quoted known and unknown prophecies. Thousands of people disposed of all their possessions, confessed their sins and calmly resigned themselves to the inevitable. Churches were crowded to overflowing; in many rural communities work was at a stand still.

Thousands, with the mysterious fate of the occupants of the Kenya Express fresh in their minds, refused to travel in trains. Soothsayers, mind readers, spiritualists and other charlatans did a rushing business. In several localities, serious revolts and riots had also occurred. The natives of Mexico had seen in the fiery visitors the symbol of their returning pagan gods, and had risen throughout the republic and had fallen upon all persons of white blood, massacring, burning, and laying waste. In India the natives had declared that the meteors were the result of the white man's radio, and had destroyed every station in the country with considerable loss of life.

Even intelligent, thinking people had let their imaginations get the better of their brains. They had promulgated and published the most far-fetched and ridiculous theories to explain a perfectly natural, if unusual, event. The editor of one widely-read and influential weekly devoted several pages of his publication to an editorial in which he sought to convince the world that the meteors were not fragments of celestial bodies attracted to Earth by its gravity, but actually were projectiles hurled at us from some other planet—presumably Mars. He quoted portions of Wells' "War of the Worlds." He pointed out that Mars was at the nearest point to Earth in many years and offered data to prove it; that every meteor that had fallen had struck Earth at a spot exactly where it might be expected to strike if it had been projected from Mars, and he confidently prophesied that the bombardment would be continued until the inhabitants of Earth had been destroyed, or until the planet had passed out of range of its neighbor.

This fantastic article brought down a storm of protesting and a deluge of assenting complimentary replies. Indeed, the intellectual public had, almost overnight, become divided into two parties: those who adhered to the Martian theory and those who did not. Politics, prohibition—all other issues—had been forgotten in the controversy over the meteors. There were cartoons, jokes, even comic pages devoted to the subject. Skits on the vaudeville stage touched upon it, and *Life* contained a humorous article scoffing at the poor marksmanship of the "Martian gunners" and calling attention to the fact that out of more than one hundred "shots," they had made no direct "bull's-eye."

As the bombardment or shower had apparently ceased, and as no great damage had been done, interest and discussion had begun to wane. Murders, holdups, and scandals had again taken their accustomed prominent places in the press, and the whole affair promised to be relegated to the limbo of the past and forgotten in a few weeks. Still, the matter was kept more or less alive. The latest papers published brief paragraphs and editorials quoting interviews with prominent scientists and endeavoring to arouse interest by calling attention to the fact that no word had been received from any of the parties that had gone in search of the fallen meteorites. I even came in for sharp criticism for not having recovered the bodies of Professor Bixby and his comrades; but on the following day the *Mercurio* retracted and explained my reasons for having made no real effort to do so.

THUS matters stood when I sailed from Chile for New York, and while the passengers and officers conversed more or less upon the recent phenomena, the more so when they discovered that I had been the first to report the initial meteorite. Still there was but slight interest in the matter. We had passed Arica and were steaming towards Mollendo. It was a lovely moonlight evening and under a galaxy of colored lights on deck the passengers were dancing to the music of the ship's orchestra. I was leaning idly upon the rail, talking with the first officer, when, glancing up, I noticed what appeared to be a fire balloon. Calling the officer's attention to it, we watched it a moment. Very rapidly it increased in size; it seemed to rush in a wide arc with terrific speed. The entire heavens were illuminated with a glare that paled the moon, our eyes were dazzled with a blinding light, and before we could turn, before we could call attention to the thing, there was a terrific report, a deafening concussion. Screams and shrieks came from the ladies; the men shouted; the musicians dropped their instruments as everyone rushed to the ship's side and with scared pale faces stared into the night. The next instant a blast of hot, evil-smelling wind swept across the ship, ripping the flag decorations from the stanchions, tipping over deck chairs like a sudden hurricane. It was over in an instant. Then, "Hold on for your lives!" bellowed an officer. Like a white wall in the moonlight a huge, foam-crested wave was rushing towards us. The ship rose on end, rolled, and gyrated. With a roar like thunder the wave struck. Hissing, seething water poured in cataracts upon the lower decks. Up-flung spray drenched us to the skin. The ship reeled, staggered, and with a shake, righted herself. A second and a third wave hurled themselves against her. But each was smaller than the preceding, and presently the vessel was again riding easily, smoothly, upon an almost calm sea.

"Close shave that!" exclaimed the officer as he rushed forward to ascertain what damage had been done. "I'll say it was!" cried a passenger. "What was it? Did you see it?"

"Another meteor," I replied, "must have struck the sea near us. It—" A sudden, terrified scream from a lady interrupted me. "Look! Look!" she shrieked. "Another!"

We rushed to the rails. Across the sky another flashing, blazing, fiery mass was rushing. For an instant we held our breaths, speechless, terrified. With a roar that was like a distant railway train, the meteor swept overhead. The sea and the ship were bathed in a green light as bright as midday. The thing receded, the light faded, and we breathed a sigh of relief. A moment later a brilliant light, like a flash of distant lightning, illuminated the southern horizon and, muffled by distance, we heard a faint detonation.

"Struck somewhere," commented a passenger. "Wonder where…?"

"Looks as if the blamed things have started again," said another. "Well, thank heavens they missed us!"

The rest of the evening was spent in talking of the event. Again discussions waxed warm, and voices rose high in the smoking-room as the men argued, theorized, contradicted and speculated. But as no more meteors fell, we rose one by one and retired.

The next morning as I stepped from the alleyway on my way to the dining saloon, I found an excited group before the wireless bulletin. "Good heavens!" I heard someone exclaim.

"Awful!" cried another.

"Heard the news, Doc?" shouted a young engineer as he caught sight of me. "That meteor last night hit Valparaiso!"

I pushed my way through the throng and gasped as I read the terrible, almost incredible news that had been radioed from Santiago. A meteor had fallen in the heart of Chile's great seaport. Practically all the city was in ruins. Buildings built upon the steep hillsides had toppled over and buried the lower portion of the city. Vessels at anchor in the harbor had been sunk or wrecked. All communication had been cut off. The city was on fire, a seething furnace, impossible to approach. At imminent risk, planes had flown near it, had circled it, and had reported the devastation. The loss of life, it was feared, was enormous. So far no survivors had been reported, no fugitives had reached the outlying towns or villages.

At last one of the meteors had hit a bull's-eye. The one chance in millions had occurred. Stunned, awed by the terrible catastrophe—brought so near because we had actually seen the meteor fall and realizing how close we had come to annihilation ourselves—we said little and ate little. Speaking in low tones, wondering what later messages would reveal, striving to convince ourselves that the ultimate investigations would reduce the losses reported, we gathered in knots and groups. But when the next radio message was received, the news was even more terrible than the first. The city was still blazing, no one had been able to enter it or approach it; but as far as known not a single inhabitant remained alive. More than this, human life had been snuffed out on every vessel in the harbor, hundreds of the inhabitants of suburbs within several miles of Valparaiso had been killed. Vina del Mar, almost a port of the city, had suffered. Crazed people were running about. Dead bodies, showing no signs of injuries, were everywhere.

And people were still dying, sinking unconscious from shock or fright.

Every effort was being made to rush aid, doctors, and supplies to the stricken district, but the electric power of the railway had been cut off, several bridges were down, and airplanes were the only means of reaching the locality.

It was terrible, ghastly, a worse disaster than the eruption of Mont Pelee in Martinique. No one could estimate the loss of life. It might be fifty thousand or one hundred thousand—perhaps more. But the destruction of Valparaiso was almost forgotten before we dined that night. That catastrophe paled into insignificance when a message was received from the Arlington radio station. It was a brief, terse message that Kansas City had been struck by still another meteorite. Once more that chance among millions had occurred. Again an aerolite, falling at random, had made a direct hit.

CHAPTER THREE

Meteorites Continue to fall

LATER news was more reassuring, however. The meteorite had done comparatively little damage to the city proper. It had struck on the outskirts, had destroyed several mills, lumberyards and hundreds of cattle, and as in the case of Valparaiso, its heat had started a conflagration. But the loss of life seemed to have been out of all proportion to the damage to property. Hundreds of people had been killed without any visible cause. They had been struck down it was assumed, by the terrific concussion of the impact, by the blast of super-heated air, or—as many eminent physicians declared—by poisonous gases generated by the molten, incandescent mass of metal.

But the worst effect, perhaps even more regrettable than the actual loss to life and property, had been the destruction of the morale of the public. Now that two cities had been hit, that hundreds or thousands of lives had been taken by the visitants, deadly fear had gripped the people. In every city and town throughout the civilized world, the inhabitants were living in momentary dread of being the next victims. It was even worse than in London during the World War and the German air raids. Then the people were subjected to attacks by fellow men, by man-made explosives. They knew more or less when the attacks were coming. They had means of combating their aerial enemies. Even if the means were inefficient, it was something they understood. But now no one knew where the next devastating meteor might strike. There was no means of avoiding them; they gave no warning. Coming from the heavens and being of more or less mysterious origin, they aroused the superstitious as well as the physical fears of the people.

Added to all this was the growing belief that they were being hurled at Earth intentionally by the inhabitants of some other sphere. This fantastic, ridiculous theory appealed to the frenzied, nervous masses. And despite the statements of scientists and the efforts of the authorities, the yellow journals played this theory to its spectacular limit.

Then another mystery was added to the matter, which had again become the absorbing topic of the world. Planes had been sent in search of the various scientific expeditions, and several had disappeared. Others had returned bringing word that they had been unable to land, but had seen the bodies of men lying about their camps, exactly as I had seen Bixby's party. And when planes had been sent to search for the missing planes, which—presumably—had crashed, they had returned with white-faced, wide-eyed men who told strange tales of seeing the missing machines standing unhurt near corpses, and with no living men on board. The question in everyone's mind was...*what had caused these deaths?* Why had everyone died who had approached a meteorite? Scores of scientists replied over the radio, through the medium of the press, by word of mouth. Gases, they declared. Unquestionably gases were given off by the molten masses. Such immense amounts of metal would require days, even weeks, to cool off. The scientists had been too impatient to investigate the things and had not taken into consideration the danger of heavy poisonous gases that might surround them. No doubt, they added, the deaths of so many apparently uninjured persons near where meteorites had struck the towns, and the deaths of those on the Kenya train, had been from these same gases.

Hereafter precautions must be taken. Everyone was warned not to approach fallen meteorites, and it was even suggested that the governments should issue gas masks to the public in anticipation of more of them falling in inhabited districts.

This was the news that came to us as we steamed northward, after the destruction of Valparaiso and the disaster at Kansas City. Nearly every day a meteor was reported from some distant part of the world or by some ship. And then the day we reached Balboa came the alarming news of fatal epidemics that had broken out in Missouri; in Chile, and in various other widely separated localities. In fact these epidemics were happening wherever a meteor had fallen in an inhabited district.

That it had some wholly inexplicable and as yet undetermined connection with the meteorites was the natural assumption, and the most prominent medical authorities openly expressed their conviction of this relation. They demanded rigid quarantines, called for volunteers to combat the rapidly spreading disease, and warned everyone to immediately move from districts where meteorites might fall. But the public—fickle as always and with that strange unaccountable antagonism for all things scientific—refused to listen. They refused to believe the aerolites had any connection with the new and malignant disease. The papers poked fun at the doctors, ridiculed them, declared it was merely their excuse, an attempt to cover up their own ignorance, and offered rewards for anyone who could advance a tenable theory as to how a mass of meteoric iron could spread any malady. The whole thing, they announced in bold headlines, was refuted by the truths of medical science. Diseases were the result of germs, of microbes. Germs could not exist when exposed even to moderate temperatures, such as that of boiling water, yet if the physicians were to be credited, masses of metal, heated to incandescence, had been germ-carriers. It was preposterous, an insult to the intelligence.

Avidly we bought copies of the *Star and Herald,* the *Panama American* and the various New York papers obtainable at Balboa, Ancon, and Panama.

No longer was the public divided into factions adhering to the Martian or non-Martian theories of the meteors' origin. Now it was the meteoric or non-meteoric origin of the epidemic, and while scientists, authorities, officials, the army and the public bickered and quarreled and argued, hundreds of people were dying each day, the doctors and nurses were being decimated, and the world was in an uproar.

The controversy had even spread to the Canal Zone. The Medical Corps was demanding a quarantine, the Engineering Corps, to which the Governor belonged, was dead against it; the civilian population was divided. An excited argument was taking place on deck as we passed through Gatun Lake. A pompous, red-faced, paunchy Colonel of Infantry was arguing with a dark, saturnine army Surgeon.

Both were on the way to the States. Someone having informed them that I was the man who had reported seeing Professor Bixby and his comrades dead upon the desert, they turned to me.

"What did *you* think?" demanded the Colonel. "What was *your* opinion of meteorites carrying some strange disease?"

"I don't pretend to think," I assured him. "I know Professor Bixby and his men, as well as his animals, are dead. I know that they were near the meteorite.

"At the time I thought it strange that they should have died of thirst. But I don't pretend to know what killed them—whether it was gas, bandits, or disease. But I'm intensely interested. The matter may solve the problem of what caused the disappearance of prehistoric American races—the Mayas, pre-Incas and others. Such a fall—or the fall of a few such meteorites with similar accompanying phenomena might—"

The Colonel haw-hawed. "Dammit!" he exclaimed, "according to this sawbones here your blasted Mayas might have come down hangin' onto the damn things. If doodlebugs can come down on a meteor, why not men? Answer that if you can, Major Waite?"

"First let me ask you a question," replied the Major. "If—"

But his question was never asked. One of the passengers came hurrying up.

"Stuttgart's gone!" he cried excitedly. "Just had a message. Not a stone left standing, every mother's son wiped out!"

At Cristobal we had confirmation of this latest and most terrible disaster. An enormous mass of incandescent matter had fallen in the heart of the ancient city. The concussion had been so terrific that glasses and windows had been shattered in Berlin, in Brussels, in Paris, and in Milan. The light, as it swept to Earth, had been dazzling from Naples to London. From points in Asia, Scotland, Egypt, had come reports of seeing the light and hearing the explosion. It was undoubtedly the largest meteor that had yet fallen, and the entire world was awed, silenced by the appalling catastrophe.

Where was this destruction to end, what city would be the next to fall? Terror reigned. What of that millionth chance? the public and the press demanded of the scientists.

The people clamored for protection, they called upon the governments to do something to avert the threatening calamity to the world, and in the next breath declared it was useless to attempt anything, as the world was doomed.

Thousands left the cities and camped in the open, seeking the comparative security of plains, woods and mountains. Law and order were rapidly vanishing. Fear, superstition and religious mania had supplanted everything else.

As we steamed across the Caribbean and up the coast, each day's news brought word of more and more terrible destruction. Genoa, Berlin, Salt Lake City, Shanghai, Adelaide, each was devastated in turn.

In the light of these fearful catastrophes—the worst in the history of the world—no one gave any heed to the innumerable meteors that struck in uninhabited districts and in the sea. Hence, to the public, unaware of these harmless falls, it appeared as if the meteorites were aimed with supernatural accuracy and diabolical cunning at the centers of civilization. And the immediate loss of life due to the things was much less than that which followed from the deadly epidemic that invariably succeeded the fall of one.

There was, however, one ray of hope—one bit of good and welcome news, in the midst of this blackness of despair. It had been proved beyond a doubt that the strange malady was not contagious. It did not spread beyond a limited area of a few square miles about the place where a meteor struck.

Doctors, nurses and others, who had gone to the assistance of stricken districts had, it is true, fallen victims to the fatal sickness, but the medical authorities pointed out that if the malady was the result of some localized effect of the meteorites, this was to be expected. And they proved beyond question that if people within the affected areas were quickly removed to other localities—even a few miles from the scene—they usually recovered and many showed no ill effects. A few died, but, as a rule, lassitude, exhaustion, sometimes delirium and at times a comatose state for a few days were followed by complete recovery.

Even the public became convinced at last that the affliction was the result of some germ or gas from the meteorites; and should one fall in their vicinity, their safety lay in hurrying from the scene instead of remaining to save their effects or the injured. Organizations were formed to see that this was done, and every city was in the condition of a town threatened with bombardment by an enemy.

Almost immediately all interests, all news, all efforts were centered on this phase of the terrible affair. No one knew when a meteor might fall, no one could forecast where it might strike; there was no way of averting them; it was a matter of chance, but the epidemic, the deaths that followed could be checked, could be fought.

Near every great city and even near the more important towns, bodies of soldiers, as well as volunteers, were stationed. They were equipped with ambulances, motor transport, and every modern device for life-saving and rapid transportation, ready to hurry all survivors from the scene in case a meteorite should strike. And every spot where a meteor had struck in or near an inhabited district was surrounded by armed troops or police to prevent anyone from approaching the danger zone.

Had it been possible to secure portions of the aerolites, scientists might have been able to discover the source of the deadly effects, and devise some means of counteracting them. But so far every attempt to secure a fragment had been futile. Several daring men had tried to approach the fallen masses, using the latest forms of gas-masks, clad in germ-proof clothes; but in every case they had been struck down and almost instantly killed before they could reach their goal.

Various devices and suggestions had been made to render the horrible death-dealing masses of metal innocuous. They had been drenched with the most powerful antiseptics and germicides, but without result.

Planes, flying above the meteorites, had dropped immense numbers of bombs whose explosions had hurled hundreds of tons of earth upon the meteors, burying them completely, and still without in the least affecting that invisible death area that extended for a mile or more in every direction.

And daily, nightly, the meteors continued to fall, sometimes singly, sometimes several at a time. Several were seen from our ship, some far distant, some uncomfortably near. The sea was fairly covered with dead fish, whales and gigantic sea-monsters from the unfathomed depths of the ocean. There were stupendous giant squids or cuttlefish, enormous octopi, and weird, horrible fishes with immense jaws. The supposed myth of the sea serpents had long since been proved the unvarnished truth. Their dead bodies had been seen floating by scores of ships, and there was not one but many species. Some were like huge overgrown eels, others were veritable serpents related to the venomous sea-snakes of the Pacific and Indian oceans, others were leftovers from prehistoric times—plesiosaurus and Ichthyosaurus-like creatures, while a few were more like gigantic turtles with small leathery shells and immensely long necks.

At any other time these creatures would have excited the wonder and interest of the world, but now, in the excitement, the panic and the mad helplessness of the people, no one gave them a passing thought. But the dead denizens of the oceans' depths were not to be lightly ignored. They formed windrows upon the shores, and presently pestilence resulted from the decomposition of the thousands of tons of rotting fish.

Armies of men were detailed to destroy them; countless millions of gallons of disinfectants were sprayed upon them. They were gathered by trainloads and burned in huge pyres.

A few ships also had been struck or destroyed by meteorites falling close to them. No one could say how many or what vessels. There was simply no time to send an SOS if a meteor swept down and annihilated a vessel with all on board. If the meteorite hit the water within a mile of the doomed ship, every soul on board perished from the gases or germs or whatever it was that surrounded the aerolites like an aura of death, and only when a vessel failed to arrive at its destined port and was posted as missing, did the world assume that it had fallen victim to the meteoric projectiles.

By the time we reached New York, half a dozen more of the world's greatest cities lay in ruins. Paris, Dublin, Leningrad, Yokohama, Benares, Cairo and Capetown. The morning after I arrived in New York, the papers announced the destruction of Buenos Aires. The following day it was Bogota. The next Rio. Then, two days without a new disaster, and then Santiago, Lima and Quito.

Suddenly some enterprising reporter made a discovery. The meteorites seemed to concentrate their fearful destructiveness on definite areas in turn. Let a city in Europe be destroyed and for several successive days other European cities would be wiped out. Then a city would be annihilated in South America and others would follow in rapid succession.

So far the United States had been particularly fortunate. Only Salt Lake City, a portion of Kansas City and some smaller towns had been destroyed. But at any time, any day, it might be our turn. And in view of this new discovery the destruction of one city would—it was believed—presage the destruction of a dozen or more.

So it was no wonder that the people were cowed with deadly fear, no wonder they could not work, could not think, could not concentrate on anything else. And so strangely does darkness affect human beings, that throughout the nights, people remained up and awake, anxiously watching the dark heavens for the brilliant light that warned of a descending meteorite, despite the fact that by far the greater number had fallen in broad daylight.

And then, on the 18th of September, the expected blow fell. Throughout the length and breadth of our country the sunlight was dimmed by the blinding, dazzling flashes of terrible light. People went mad with the thundering reverberations of falling aerolites, the terrifying concussions as they struck Earth. On every side flames and dense clouds of smoke arose; the earth was torn up; forests were leveled by dozens of the gigantic meteorites, and when at last the bombardment ceased, more than one hundred thousand lives had been lost. San Francisco, Richmond, Detroit, Springfield, Buffalo, New Haven, Concord, Saratoga, Dayton, Trenton, Atlanta, Biloxi, Tucson, Dallas, Denver, and Seattle were in ruins.

So terrific, so overwhelming, so indescribable was the loss of life and property, that only a brief paragraph in the papers reported the fact that the Panama Canal had been completely destroyed, that Gatun Lake had been transformed to a vast, muddy, pestilential plain, that thousands of men, women and children had been killed upon the Isthmus.

Everyone—even the most conservative—now believed the end of the world had come. All hope was abandoned. In the face of such a catastrophe, human beings were helpless. All who had means sought to escape from the accursed land. Every available ship in every remaining port was filled to overflowing with refugees, fleeing they knew not where, seeking wildly, hopelessly to reach some spot where the blazing destroyers would not strike.

But they were no better off than those who, resigning themselves to fate or unable to flee, remained at home. Dozens of the ships vanished with all their human freight. A few were sighted, derelict, floating aimlessly with their decks littered with dead. Only a few ever reached port. Even the bravest, the stoutest-hearted began to abandon all hope. Even, the most optimistic were overwhelmed. Could it be that the end was really near?

CHAPTER FOUR
An Astounding Discovery

IT was at this crisis, at this time when the world seemed a chaos, when civilization seemed doomed to be wiped from the face of the Earth, when everyone was aghast, numbed, and helpless in the face of such a stupendous, overwhelming catastrophe, that Paul Henderson appeared upon the scene. One day he was an inconspicuous citizen, a man scarcely known outside his own circle of family, friends, and business associates. The next he was the most famed, most widely known, most discussed man in the entire world. In every country every newspaper blazoned his name, hundreds of millions of people were familiar with his face and features. From an amateur scientist and obscure author who wrote imaginative fiction based on fact ("sugar-coated pills of science" one reviewer called his stories), he rose overnight to worldwide prominence, to be hailed as the savior of Earth.

An article in the *New York Times* had accomplished the miracle.

Quietly, unobtrusively he had been working for weeks along unique and original lines. He had formulated a theory. He had experimented, tested, investigated, until he had convinced himself that his theory was correct. And then and not until then did he call on the editor of the paper, expound his theory, relate the story of his activities, and give a summary of the results.

A special edition of the paper had published the astounding news. So important did the editor consider the article that instead of making a "killing" with the scoop, he had transmitted it to every paper, every news syndicate, and every press organization throughout the world. He also made immediate arrangements to have it broadcast from every radio station that still remained in operation.

Henderson, at risk of his own life, had secured samples of the meteorites. That he had succeeded in doing so (by using safeguards designed by himself and adapted to his theory) had proved the truth of his theory. The deadly character of the meteorites, he said, was not due to gas nor to germs. It was the result of a hitherto unknown ray, or a vibratory wave, a discharge of electrons from the meteors. This in itself was an entirely new and revolutionary theory.

Confident that he was right, he had devised a costume and a mask that were impervious to all known rays, and had ventured cautiously within the danger zone of a large meteor that had fallen in the Adirondacks.

He had felt no ill effects, and a few days later had approached even nearer the thing. This time he had felt ill. He had experienced a roaring in his ears, partial blindness, and other alarming symptoms. He had, however, quickly recovered, and realizing that his costume was not proof against the discharge from the meteor, he had devoted several weeks to improving it. Then he had once more approached the mass. This time he had felt no effects, he had actually reached the meteorite, and with the greatest difficulty, had chiseled off a small portion. For several days thereafter he had been prostrated, but no sooner had he recovered than he had buried himself in his laboratory studying, testing, and experimenting with the only known specimen of the aerolites that had worked such havoc and destruction with the world.

His results confirmed his theory. The bit of meteorite emitted a new ray, a terrific discharge of waves. Placing it near a live rabbit he had seen the creature die, had dissected it, had spent days and nights making a microscopic examination of its vital organs and tissues. He had determined conclusively that the brain was affected, that the discharge from the piece of meteorite completely altered the molecular structure of the brain, that it upset or disintegrated the arrangement of the molecules, perhaps of the atoms and their electrons.

"But," to quote the article in the *Times*, "Mr. Henderson was not yet satisfied. He had risked his life to secure the sample by means of which he had established the validity of his theory. He had convinced himself of the cause of death—the action of the fatal ray. However, could he be sure that all the meteors possessed the same characters and emitted the same rays?

"Once more this daring young man took his life in his hands and entered the dread area of death surrounding another meteor. If his hypothesis was correct, if all of them were alike, he was safe, for he had perfected his ray-proof costume until tests with the fragment he had secured had proved it one hundred percent resistant.

"But if he was wrong, if the ray or the vibratory waves from this second meteor varied in the slightest from the first, he would have sacrificed his life for the cause of humanity. The world may be thankful that he was right.

"He secured more specimens, continued his tests and experiments, and now is positive that his theory is the correct one; that, equipped with his devices, human beings will be immune to the deadly rays.

"Moreover, he has discovered that animals, even then apparently dead from the effects of the ray, may be revived and show no indications of ill effects. This Mr. Henderson accomplishes by means of a powerful electric current so designed as to create a vibratory wave of incredibly high periodicity, which appears to have the property of reorganizing the disarranged brain cells.

"We believe, and we are confident that the public will believe, that Mr. Henderson has made the most important discovery of modern times. And like every epochal discovery, it is extremely simple.

"It is in fact astounding that among all our so-called scientists, our medical men, our technical experts, nobody had thought of a deadly ray or emanation of ions as the basis of the fatal area about the meteorites, and the more so as the death-dealing discharge from radioactive minerals is so well-known. So many unfortunate deaths have, in the past, occurred from so-called radium poisoning—the destructive action on tissues and bones of radium discharges, that the public is thoroughly familiar with the deadly character of radioactive minerals. We are indeed surprised—now that Mr. Henderson has announced his truly remarkable discovery—that some scientist did not suggest that the celestial destroyers might contain radium in sufficient quantities to cause death to human beings. That no such theory was advanced was doubtless due to the fact that this new ray, discovered by Mr. Henderson, acts only upon the brain and leaves no trace that is discernible to the naked eye.

"Although Mr. Henderson's discovery does not relieve the world of the constant fear of descending meteors; though it does not aid us in combating these irresistible agents of destruction; though it does not throw any light upon their origin or cause, it will yet be the means of saving hundreds of thousands of lives. As is generally known, the loss of life through the immediate and direct contact of the meteorites is comparatively small as compared to the loss of life resulting from the hitherto mysterious emanations from them after they have fallen.

"Not only will Mr. Henderson's discoveries enable us to entirely counteract and overcome this deplorable sacrifice of lives, but it will enable us to save those who are struck down by the rays. Mr. Henderson is the greatest benefactor of the human race in countless centuries. He has most providentially come forward when every effort, every attempt to mitigate these worldwide disasters have failed. He has been the direct means of saving millions of human lives. Gratitude, thanks and honor to Mr. Henderson should fill every human heart throughout the entire world.

"We call upon our officials and our governments immediately to provide every citizen with the ray-proof equipment designed by Mr. Henderson. We demand it. The public, humanity, demands it. Every hour, every moment of delay means loss of life, the loss of perhaps thousands of lives.

"No human power can control the descending meteors. Tonight or tomorrow one may destroy Washington, New York, or London. To delay is not only dangerous, it is criminal. Every official, every man who opposes such a measure, who does not exert all his efforts to protect the human race from imminent destruction, is a potential if not an actual murderer.

"Let the public rise and insist. Let every mill, every factory, every laboratory, every resource of every country be devoted entirely to the manufacture of ray-proof equipment and the resuscitating devices of Mr. Henderson; *the* man of the hour, *the* man of the century."

FOR once, wonder of wonders, the governments acted. For once in the world's history there was no arguing, no conferring, no slow unwinding of red tape. Politics, diplomacy, budgets, authority everything that would hinder immediate action was scrapped. For once the officials and the executives realized that whatever was done must be done at once. Every resource was, as the *Times* had demanded, as the public now demanded, devoted to turning out the Henderson outfits.

But progress was necessarily slow. The materials were scarce, the utmost care had to be used, new machines had to be devised, and though the outfits were produced at the rate of thousands a day, there were millions of people to be equipped. And a tremendous problem arose as to their distribution. It had been internationally agreed by all nations that the outfits should not be sold, that they should be given free to the inhabitants, that there should be no restrictions, no duties on them or any of the materials used in making them. The whole world was working day and night to save humanity, the whole world was for once united in a common cause.

But to distribute the outfits to some individuals and not to all would be considered as discrimination. Those without them would be exposed to death while those equipped would be immune. Riots would result, revolutions, war. The only solution was to wait until enough outfits were ready to equip every inhabitant of a city at once, and to take the cities in the order of their size and importance.

Naturally this aroused controversy, ill feeling, and mad protests. An unimportant town was as liable to be struck as a great city. The people pointed out that New York, Boston, London, Rome, Madrid and other capitals still remained untouched, while scores of lesser cities lay in smoldering ruins. Why, they demanded, should they be exposed to death, while others were comparatively safe?

But the cooler-headed, more rational-minded prevailed. The great cities, they pointed out, were more important. If their inhabitants were destroyed there would be no hope for the others, as there would be a curtailment, if not a cessation, of the manufacture of the outfits.

Meanwhile, the Henderson resuscitating apparatus had gone rapidly ahead. These machines were easily made. They could be produced by the same machines and the same workmen as many other electrical appliances.

Within a month of the announcement of Mr. Henderson's discovery, every city and town in America and Europe was provided with one or more of the devices—the number varying according to the population of the city. This did much to calm the people. If worst came to the worst those who survived could revive the others. And as each city and town was provided with a corps of specially trained men, equipped with ray-proof outfits—whose duty it was to operate the resuscitating apparatus in case of need—the public regained some confidence.

Meanwhile, Mr. Henderson had been deluged with honors, with decorations and with degrees and titles. The initials he was entitled to place after his name would have covered half a page if written out. He was a Sir, a Chevalier, a Professor, a Doctor, a Knight, a Marquis, a Duke, an Hidalgo and a score of other exalted personages all in one. Gifts varying from motor cars to mansions, from clothing to castles had been pressed upon him. An honorary position with an attendant salary almost equal to the President's had been voted him by his own Government. Foreign potentates and powers had done even more.

But he scarcely realized all this. The meteors were still falling. City after city and town after town were being destroyed throughout the world, and while the loss of life, thanks to Henderson's discoveries, had been minimized, still thousands were being killed, billions of dollars worth of property were being destroyed, and the discoverer of "Henderson's Rays" worked day and night on a new theory, on a new hypothesis.

He had found how to protect human beings from the deadly rays of the meteorites, could he not find a means of protecting the world from the meteorites themselves?

It seemed on the face of it an impossible task, a dream, something far beyond human possibility. But he was not the type of man to whom anything appeared impossible. No one was more appreciative than Henderson of the marvels of science; no one was a greater believer in its future developments and wonders. For years he had been accustomed to dream of that future, to imagine accomplishments beyond the dreams of ordinary men, to visualize seemingly miraculous and impossible events, and then to explain them, to produce them along scientific lines in his stories.

Here, ready-made, an actuality, he had a theme, a plot, a situation more dramatic, more intense, more terrible and far more mysterious and insoluble than anything he had ever imagined in his wildest fancies. Could he not, he asked himself, treat it like one of those fancies? Could he not work out, little by little, the details, logically correlate the facts, as he would the ideas in a story, and reason from effect to cause? And once he placed his finger—or his mind rather—upon the cause, would it not be possible to find a remedy? He believed it would. He had followed the same method in his successful explanation of the fatal effect of the meteorites. If it worked in one case, why shouldn't it in another?

He shut himself up, concentrated his mind, cudgeled his brain. He covered hundreds of sheets of paper with notes, data, possibilities, the wildest of fancies and suppositions. And slowly, gradually, out of the mass of thoughts, conjectures, reasoning, facts, data and theories, certain undeniable truths emerged.

Coincidences—the ever-handy and useful accessories of fiction writers—had, he knew, their limits.

Coincidences did not repeat themselves over and over again. They were the exception rather than the rule. Could it be that a coincidence could account for so many cities being struck when there was so much more unoccupied territory where they might have fallen? He mentally decided no.

Admitting this, could the laws of chance or coincidence explain the indisputable fact, that there were well-marked cycles of meteor-falls, that each of these bombardments, so to say, was largely centered upon a definite and rather restricted area of Earth's surface? Again he shook his head. Granted that it was not chance, not coincidence, then what was it?

If Earth were passing through an enormous meteoric area, if it were passing through the tail of a comet, if it were passing through a dark nebula, as the scientists claimed, it might account for the periodic showers, but it could not account for the other facts that he had decided were not explicable by laws of chance. Meteorites, striking Earth during such a passage, would of necessity strike here, there, and everywhere. The Earth was whirling about on its axis; it was rushing along on its orbit. Falling meteorites, if left to chance, would pepper its surface indiscriminately. There was not one chance in millions—he recalled the confident words of the astronomers—that they would strike buildings or towns, there were still more remote chances that they would strike several towns the same day or night, and there were still more slender chances of their striking several towns in one portion of Earth's surface.

And yet—he referred to his carefully tabulated data—of all the thousands of meteorites that had been reported, fully twenty percent had made hits on towns, cities or thickly inhabited districts. Still more remarkable was the fact that many had struck ships at sea. What, he wondered, were the mathematical chances of a falling meteorite striking a moving vessel?

For a few moments he worked rapidly, covering a sheet of paper with figures. At the result he dropped his pencil and whistled. He had taken the area of Long Island Sound, had added up the combined areas of the decks of all the vessels that, normally, should be upon the Sound, at one time, and the result astounded him. Even in such a small-congested body of water, the area of water compared with the deck area of shipping was almost infinite. What must it be on the vast expanse of the mighty oceans? The human brain could scarcely conceive it. It would be one chance is billions that a vessel would be hit!

"No!" he exclaimed jumping from his chair, lighting his pipe and pacing the room excitedly. "It is not chance. It cannot be. And if the meteorites are not guided by chance, then of a certainty, they must be guided by something, by some power, some purpose, some intelligence! I am sure of it. But who will believe it? And whence do they come? Who, what, is the power that is hurling these terrific, awful projectiles at Earth?"

CHAPTER FIVE
Professor Henderson's Conclusions

ALTHOUGH Mr. Henderson (he disliked intensely being referred to as Chevalier Sir Don Paul Henderson, Marquis de Givanni, Duque de Zaragon, etc., etc.) possessed a far from superficial knowledge of most sciences, there was one of which he knew very little. This was astronomy, and it was astronomy upon which he must depend largely in his present needs. But if he was not a practical astronomer himself, still he had at his disposal all the astronomical notes, observations and data that had been written or published regarding the meteorites, from the time or the first one that had fallen in Chile. And he felt quite confident that by tabulating, correlating, and studying these, he could bring some order out of the astronomical chaos, and could arrive at some definite conclusion.

It was at this time that I first became acquainted with him. We met at the home of a mutual friend, and were soon conversing earnestly. Perhaps it was the fact that I had reported the first of the meteors, or it may have been my interest in the phenomena, or the fact that I was something of a theorist and a scientific iconoclast myself that attracted him. But at all events he evidently took an immediate liking to me, a feeling that I reciprocated. From that moment we were fast friends. I spent a great deal of time with him and—so I flatter myself—my suggestions and ideas helped him considerably in his work. But I do not wish to take any of the credit that rightfully and wholly belongs to him.

He was also greatly interested in and considerably impressed with my theory that the mysterious and abrupt termination of prehistoric American cultures might have been caused by a similar meteoric visitation in past ages.

"But," he objected when I first mentioned and explained this to him, "if the civilizations had been wiped out by meteorites, why have no traces of such meteors ever been found? They would be as enduring as the stone sculptures."

"That," I replied, "has always been one of the strongest arguments against the theory, but your own discovery has done away with it. Ordinary meteorites are, we know, practically indestructible and will remain practically unaltered for immeasurable periods of time.

"But these aerolites are not of the ordinary type. You have proved that they are continuously emitting showers of radiant energy, perhaps of ions, and this discharge must of necessity result either in the decomposition or in the diminution of the original mass. This is an unalterable law of nature, and while the loss to radium, for example, is so slight as scarcely to be detectable, the loss in the case of these meteoric masses may be extremely rapid.

"In that case, is it not probable that any meteors—similar or identical with these—which may have fallen in past ages, would have completely disintegrated and disappeared in a few thousand years?"

"Well, I hadn't thought of that!" he exclaimed. "It will be interesting to find out. I'll weigh the pieces I have and we'll soon see."

The result of the tests was to prove conclusively that the shrinkage of the material was, comparatively speaking, very rapid. The fragments in Henderson's laboratory had already lost nearly one ten-thousandth of their original weight.

"I guess you're right," he declared. "At that rate the decrease would be approximately one thousandth a year, and a one-thousand-ton meteor would disappear completely in ten centuries. Now I wonder—but of course there is no way to prove it—I was wondering if there haven't been regularly recurring cycles of these falls. You see, if there have been such, it would explain a lot of mysterious things in the past—all those old prophecies and legends—Sodom and Gomorrah, Earth being destroyed by fire, the end of civilizations, the inexplicable exodus and migration of entire races, even perhaps the glacial period. And it might explain where these things originate, where they come from.

"It's a darned pity…" He sighed regretfully, "…that there weren't scientists and astronomers in those days, so we could look up the records."

I laughed. "You're not very complimentary to the astronomers," I said. "I notice you draw a distinction between them and scientists."

Henderson grinned. "No, I didn't mean it that way," he said. "I have the greatest respect for astronomers as astronomers. I only wish I knew more about astronomy myself. But you know, Merritt, the more I go through these notes and figures, the more I'm amazed to discover how little real study the astronomers have devoted to meteors. Of course they saw them and watched them, but there doesn't appear to have been any concerted, systematized and comparative observations made.

"Here, for example..." He picked up a sheet of notes. "...are all the known reports and observations made on the night of August 31st. It is known positively that seven meteorites fell on that night, and yet no one, working solely from astronomical observations, could determine how many fell.

"One observer—in California—mentions seeing 'several' large meteorites, some of which unquestionably struck Earth's surface. He goes a bit farther and records the positions of two when first observed, the rate of their progress, their parabolas and their comparative size. Then the chap down in Arequipa, Peru, mentions seeing 'five meteors.' He must have completely missed two, and he 'believes' three of them struck Earth.

"He also reported the time he observed them and gives the position of one, but he doesn't state whether the time and position were when he first saw them or after they had been rushing through space for some time. The old fellow in Texas is the champion, however. He reports seeing *nine* meteors and he got so excited over it that he completely forgot to note their location or the time. Now what can you make of that?"

I shook my head. Then a brilliant idea came to me. "I take it," I said, "that your effort is to prove whether these meteorites are natural falls—the chance visitors from some dark cosmic space of meteoric character through which we are passing—or are being projected at us from some other planet with malice aforethought?"

He nodded.

"In order to do this," I continued, "you are trying to get some sort of tabulated, comparative data from astronomical observations. But you find that—despite the fact that the meteorites were the most important things in the universe—the stargazers were far more interested in working out their own fads and foibles than in checking up on the meteorites."

"Righto!" he assented.

"In that case," I again continued, "isn't it possible that you might get results by finding out exactly what these self-centered astronomers were so intently watching on the nights when the meteors fell? If, for example, you found that half a dozen men all had their telescopes focused on the moon, and that all or the majority of these six men reported—even casually—that seven meteors had fallen on the night of August 31st, and if you found that six other astronomers had been watching other planets or constellations and that a majority of these men had failed to record the full number, wouldn't it prove that the things come from some point in the direction of the moon?"

Henderson rubbed his chin thoughtfully at this.

"And if you found that, night after night, the same held true, wouldn't it tend to prove that all had a common origin? On the other hand, if on different days they came from different points, wouldn't it tend to prove the reverse? And you could check up on your conclusions by finding exactly where the seven hit, whether, taking into consideration Earth's angle, its rotation, and the reported position of the meteors, they struck where they might have been expected, if they had come from the assumed direction."

He sprang to his feet and clapped me on the back enthusiastically. "Who says two heads are not better than one!" he cried. "That's a bully idea. Now we can get somewhere!"

"And there's another matter that has occurred to me," I reminded him. "A lot of the meteorites have fallen in the daytime. You can find out if any of these were mentioned by astronomers, just where they had their telescopes focused, and thus prove fairly conclusively from what direction the daytime meteors fell. And if that checks up with the altered position of Earth in its rotation, and if the things struck where they might have been expected in relation to the altered position of Earth's surface, you can be positive that you are on the right track."

"Merritt!" he exclaimed. "I never would have believed an archeologist had so much—"

"Common sense—" I suggested with a laugh.

"Nooo...not that," he grinned. "But such a grasp of matters entirely outside his own particular—well, science."

"An archeologist," I informed him, "finds logical reasoning and roundabout methods the shortest road to reaching desired goals. We, you must remember, seldom have any real facts or data to work on. Instead of unraveling puzzles by deciphering inscriptions, we must in nine cases out of ten decipher the inscriptions by first unraveling the puzzles. And you must also remember that archeology is hardly a science. It is a combination of many sciences—to be a good archeologist one must be a geographer, a geologist, a botanist, a naturalist, an engineer, an anatomist, a philologist, a zoologist, an ethnologist, a paleontologist, and several other ologists. And, preeminently, one must be a theorist and must possess a vivid imagination. You, my friend, would make a most excellent and eminent archeologist."

"And if I, or someone else, don't get at the bottom of this mystery and find how to get the better of these meteors, there won't be any need of anyone but archeologists in a short time," he declared. "Do you know," he continued, "that at the present rate, if this destruction continues, every town and city on Earth will have peen utterly destroyed within the next fifty years?"

I gasped. "No, I didn't," I admitted. "But," I said, "is it possible that these meteors can continue to fall at the present rate for the next fifty, even for the next two years?"

"I don't see why not," he replied. "If they are natural, and we are passing through a vast aggregation of them—through a disrupted star as Professor Dutcher claims—they might continue for fifty or one hundred or more years; they may fill hundreds of thousands of miles of space. And if they are being hurled at us from some other planet, if we are being bombarded by the damnable things with the intention of destroying us, they'll continue to come until our enemies on the planet have exhausted their ammunition or have succeeded in their devilish design."

"Do you honestly believe that is the solution?" I asked.

He nodded. "Yes," he declared. "And why not?" he continued. "All thinking people are convinced that the planets are inhabited by rational beings of some sort or another. In all probability—considering the age and the environments and the conditions of those planets—their inhabitants are immeasurably ahead of us poor humans in every way. It seems like the wildest sort of fiction to think of the denizens of one planet bombarding a neighbor, hundreds of thousands—even millions of miles distant. But it would have seemed fully as much like impossible fiction had I or anyone else, previous to 1914, suggested that human beings could hurl explosive shells at an enemy fifty miles distant. It would have seemed just as preposterous to have suggested, twenty years ago, that not only human speech but moving life-like images of human beings could be transmitted through the air across the Atlantic.

"What is impossible fiction, preposterous, today is everyday fact tomorrow. Why, Merritt, if two years or even a year ago I had written a story describing how Earth was wiped out, how every vestige of civilization was destroyed by meteors, would anyone have believed it possible?"

"No," I admitted, "they would not. It doesn't seem possible to me yet. In fact, I think it is that feeling of unreality—that feeling that it can't last—that has made the people as a whole act in the way they do and have done. If it hadn't been for you, Henderson, half the population of Earth would have been annihilated before now. And even now you're the only man in the world who is really working along lines that may result in any real benefit or may bring a cessation of this horror."

Henderson flushed. "Oh, that was just fate," he insisted. "You see I'd written a story once—a long time ago in fact—in which I used the discharges from a radioactive mineral to destroy people. Naturally, when people began to die mysteriously in the vicinity of the meteors, I thought of my story. But you know I don't believe in this case that it's a discharge of ions or rays as you may call them, that's the cause of the deaths."

"What!" I cried. "Why, I thought that was precisely what you *did* believe—what you had proved. Why, your entire life-saving and protective apparatus was based on that belief…"

"Not exactly," he replied. "I did at first think so, I admit. But if you read the first article on my findings, you'll see that I said that I believed and had proved that death resulted from some unknown ray, discharge or waves. And I've pretty well proved to my own satisfaction that it's waves—some sort of electro-magnetic waves. And what's more…" He became very earnest. "…I'm convinced that the waves do not originate in the meteorites!"

"Then for heaven's sake where do they originate?" I demanded. "You say they emanate from the things, but don't originate there. You're talking in contradictions, Henderson."

"No, I'm not," he declared. "When you listen in on a receiving set and hear sounds brought to you by radio waves, do those waves originate in the set?"

"Of course not," I replied, "they originate in the transmitting apparatus."

"Exactly!" exclaimed Henderson, "and that, I am sure, is where the deadly waves from these meteorites originate—in the transmitting apparatus on another planet!"

"Good lord!" I ejaculated, "you mean that you think these horrible things are not only hurled at us as projectiles, but are capable of receiving and then transmitting waves that destroy human life?"

"That's precisely what I do believe," he replied.

"But why?" I asked. "Why shouldn't the inhabitants of whatever planet it is (if it is any) turn their rays on us directly? Why go to all that roundabout method?"

"For the same reason that we humans do not transmit our sound waves and power waves directly, without going through the roundabout method of transforming sound waves to electro-magnetic waves, transmitting the latter, and then, in a receiving apparatus, transforming them back to sound waves again. In other words my theory is that the death waves cannot be transmitted through space—at least for any great distance—but that they can be superimposed upon, or transformed into, some other type of waves, and that these transmitted through space, are received, transformed to death rays and are discharged—perhaps tremendously amplified by the meteorites."

"But," I objected, loath to admit such a revolutionary and terrible hypothesis could be true. "To accomplish anything of that sort would require a complicated, delicate piece of mechanism, while these meteors are masses of solid metal—molten, incandescent, almost fluid, when they pass through our atmosphere and strike Earth. How can any mass of metal do any of the things you suggest?"

"That's a question no one can answer," admitted Henderson, "anymore than anyone can explain why a lot of natural things—minerals, metals, and salts—possess the properties they do. Why, I might ask, are some minerals and metals magnetic and some non-magnetic? Why is it possible to weld or alloy two particular metals and not others? Why do certain minerals always crystallize in the same complex forms while others vary enormously? Why are nine hundred and ninety-nine thousand out of one million snails' shells right-hand coiled? Why are no two leaves, no two blades of grass, no two hairs on all the human heads in the world precisely alike? Why should Rochelle salt crystals possess such almost uncanny properties of amplifying sound? Why should—but what's the use? I might just as well ask why is a mouse? and be done with it.

"No one knows the why. We simply know certain things are and make use of them and that's all. And the devils who are trying to wipe out the civilization of our old planet are making use of powers and properties of substances of which we know nothing—and they're succeeding too blamed well. It's up to us, Merritt, to get busy and stop 'em. You can't make me believe there isn't a way, and you can't convince me yet that human brains are not as good as, if not better than, the brains of any monstrosities that may be patting themselves on the back up on Mars or Venus or somewhere else."

"I'm afraid I won't be of much use," I said, "but I'll be only too glad to help all I can. Why can't we organize a corps—an army, a multitude of men, to work together on this problem? If two heads are better than one, two hundred or two thousand or two million should be just so many more times better."

"No use," he declared with finality. "I've tried it, the papers have tried it. What's the result? Discussions, controversies, ill feelings among the scientists. They won't work together. Each has his pet hobby; each is jealous of the others or ridicules him. And they all go off on tangents. Get so damned interested in their own particular line of research that they forget everything else.

"I tell you, Merritt, that the average professional scientist is the most impractical, pig-headed, narrow-minded, self-centered, unimaginative man on Earth. And when it comes to an emergency, he gets as rattled, as confused and as nervous as an old woman. And he's so darned absent-minded. Take old Professor McCurdy, when New Haven was hit, and he was lucky enough to escape, being just outside the danger zone, what did he do? Did he try to get away, to get others away, to help the injured? Not a bit of it! He just stood there, wringing his hands, bemoaning the loss of his books and notes, until some one dragged him off.

"I admire scientists' brains. I admit their attainments. I agree that they have been instrumental in giving the world its most remarkable and useful things. But that was in spite of them, not because of them. How many inventions, of any real value have ever been made by scientists? How many have seen the commercial value or the practical importance of their discoveries? And the Lord alone knows how many discoveries they have made, that might be of value to humanity, but which have been forever lost and buried because the discoverers couldn't see beyond their own noses."

I raised my eyebrows at this.

"Maybe you think I'm knocking science," he continued, "but I'm not. Science is the biggest thing in the world; it's the key to everything, but it's inefficiently run, and no machine or anything else can do its best if it's not operated efficiently. Gosh, Merritt, I ought to know! My father was a scientist and a darned good one.

"You father?" I asked.

"Yes." He replied. "I was brought up on scientists and science. But my father died a poor man, though a lot of ignorant, thick-headed men, who couldn't have told the difference between a diatom and a mastodon if they were to die for it, made millions out of patenting inventions based on his discoveries."

"Sometimes scientists can be very impractical," I interjected. "Especially about money."

He nodded in agreement and continued, "But the worst of all is that scientists won't believe anything they haven't proved. And yet the whole history of science proves that about as fast as some scientist proved a thing, another proved something that disproved the other chap's proof. You'd think scientists—knowing the almost unlimited possibilities of science itself—would be the greatest of visionaries. But they're not. They refuse to believe that this, that, or the other can be or may happen, because they haven't proved it can or may.

"Why, I remember when I was at Yale, we were taught in our class on geology that petroleum could only exist in carboniferous rocks! I remember the ridicule that was aroused when wireless telegraphy was suggested. But you know all those things yourself. And what did the scientists say about these meteors? That there wasn't a chance in millions of a city being hit. That the 'shower' would be of short duration. And, up-to-date…" He referred to his notes. "…up-to-date 718 meteors have been recorded, and ninety-two important cities and one hundred and thirty-three towns and villages have been hit—nearly one-third of the meteors have struck towns. And that doesn't include ships that have been destroyed at sea. And instead of being of 'brief duration' the damnable things have been coming down regularly for the past eleven weeks! Yet, if I should announce that the things come from some planet, if I should make public my theory of the death-waves, every Tom, Dick, and Harry of a scientist would scoff at me, call me a charlatan, a scare-head and an ignoramus or worse. And—"

"I admit a lot you say is true," I interrupted, "but how about the practical men, the imaginative men like yourself; the hundreds, thousands of men who must exist, who have a knowledge of scientific matters, who are broad-minded and willing to work on a theory, no matter how extravagant, and who could work in conjunction with you?"

"They're most likely all too busy with other matters," declared Henderson. "There's a tremendous amount of reconstruction, of reorganization of everything else going on as you know. And this is a one-man job—or at least a two-man job. A crowd would only befog things, I'm afraid. Everyone would have slightly different theories and ideas; they'd work on individual lines, and we'd get into a confused mess. You see, Merritt, the way I look at a theory—especially if it's a wild and seemingly impossible one—is that it's a kind of inspiration. It gets into a fellow's head, a sort of premonition or hunch or something, and he's got to work it out himself. Of course, a friend like you is a big help. You don't offer some other theory that may influence mine. You accept mine, but, as it's not a child of your brain, you can see a lot of holes in it—weak spots—and can offer suggestions and ideas about working it out. You've given me a lot of tips already. Now I'm going to get busy on checking up on what all those astronomers were doing, when they were too busy to notice meteors that—for all they knew—might knock them and their telescopes into powder the next minute. Do you know," he chuckled, "they remind me of the artist who was sketching in the Rockies. A big grizzly came rampaging along, and almost knocked over his easel. A few moments later, a hunter appeared. 'Seen a bear?' he asked. 'I'm not interested in natural history,' replied the other, 'I'm an artist. A beast of some sort most seriously interfered with my work, however. Possibly it was a bear.'"

"'How long ago?' demanded the hunter. 'Where did he go?'"

"'My dear fellow,' exclaimed the artist irritably, 'How do you imagine I can concentrate my brain on the shadow tones of that canyon and be cognizant of the exact hour and minute of an event which was a confounded nuisance? And I hope he's gone to the devil and that you'll follow him.'"

CHAPTER SIX
Hurled from Mars

I LEFT Henderson deep in his researches and calculations. He was, I thought to myself, a most remarkable man, an undoubted genius, a man whose brain was not only a veritable storehouse of the widest, most diversified general knowledge, but capable of drawing upon that vast accumulated knowledge when needed. Yet he was quite capable of ignoring all the facts of this knowledge, and soaring—unimpeded—into the greatest heights of fancy and imagination.

I chuckled to myself as I recalled his tirade against scientists. If ever there was a true scientist he was one himself. But I realized there was only too much truth in what he had said. And I could not blame him, could not blame anyone for being rather disgusted with the behavior of scientists—or I might better say scientific specialists, in the terrible crisis through which the world had been passing for the last eleven weeks. They had fallen down completely. Not a single statement or promise they had made had been borne out. They had by their own disagreements and contradictions, tacitly admitted they were at an entire loss, and yet they had refused to listen to or to consider any suggestions or theories of others.

Even when Henderson had come forward with his theory supported by obvious and incontrovertible proofs, they had been loath to admit that he was right. He had been praised, honored, and rewarded by the public, by governments, almost at once—but the scientific bodies had been the very last to recognize what he had done. Even now I knew there were many scientists who refused to admit that he was right.

He was a modest man. He did not know the meaning of conceit; but, like all modest and rather shy and retiring men, he was very sensitive, very easily hurt, and while he showed no disposition to boast of what he had done, still he fully realized it and naturally resented the attitude of many professional men towards him.

And I fully appreciated the fact that, were he to broadcast his present apparently wild and impossible theory, he would be laughed at and ridiculed. That I felt sure, was why he would not listen to my suggestion of enlisting the cooperation of others in trying to work out his theory. He was afraid, if it proved untenable, of the 'I-told-you-sos' that would result. It certainly did seem like a preposterous idea, and yet, somehow, I had a feeling that Henderson was right.

It was not as I have already said, the first time that it had been suggested that the meteors were being projected at Earth from another planet, and there were countless thousands of persons who still believed in that theory. But as the weeks had gone on, interest in that side of the matter had waned. Indeed, the attitude of the public, the reactions of the masses, had undergone a complete alteration.

At first there had been wild panic, crazed terror, nerve-racking suspense. The whole world had been disordered, upset, disorganized. But, so adaptable is man to his environment that in a surprisingly short space of time, people had become more or less accustomed to the unprecedented conditions. Just as, in the days of the World War, people became inured to gun fire, to air raids, to hearing of thousands of men mowed down in a single attack, although during times of peace the world would stand aghast at a railway accident with the loss of a score of lives, so now the people regarded the daily destruction of a town, and the almost constant flashing, detonating discharges from the sky, as everyday events.

A few weeks earlier, the news of a meteorite striking a town was announced by glaring headlines in special editions of the papers, crowds gathered and in frightened excited tones discussed the disaster, and people lived in constant dread. But now, unless the town was a most important city, a column or less would be devoted to it; it scarcely aroused comment on the streets, and people lived, went about their business and slept as soundly as though the world were quite normal.

But Henderson's revelations as to the rate of destruction had astounded me. How many people, how many officials, I wondered, were aware of this? It might be better for everyone that the public was now calm, complacent and blissfully devoid of worry over where the next aerolite would fall.

And towns and cities were constantly being rebuilt with a sublime confidence that—like lightning—meteorites would not strike twice in the same spot. But if Henderson was right—and I felt confident he was—the destruction was exceeding the construction. If the meteors continued to fall, it would be only a question of time before—as he had said—the world would be in ruins.

It was an appalling thought, the more so perhaps because the devastation was proceeding so gradually that it was not obvious. It was like some terrible, incurable disease—like slow paralysis. And like paralysis, there would come a day when, with a start and a shock, the world would come to a sudden realization that it was doomed. Perhaps it was largely realization of this inexorably slow but sure fate, that convinced me that Henderson was right—that there was a malicious, definite, carefully planned purpose in the meteorite bombardment.

It did not seem possible that mere chance could have resulted in this. And then there was the amazing percentage of hits, something that I had never realized until Henderson had given me the figures. Nearly thirty-three and one-third per cent of the meteorites had struck towns! I remembered that humorous article in *Life*. *P*oor marksmanship! Good Lord, the meteors were making a better record of hits than any gun-crew in the United States Navy! That alone ought to convince the most skeptical. Chance meteors could not by any possibility do that.

No, beyond a doubt, I decided, the things were being hurled at us from some other planet, and hurled or fired with the most amazing accuracy. What masterminds must be behind the guns, so to say, to be able to fire thousand-ton masses of metal through hundreds of thousands of miles of space and strike such infinitesimal targets as cities covering a few square miles of Earth's surface!

And what hope had human beings of escaping from such superhuman beings? What chance had we to compete with them, to outwit them, even to defy them? And that mysterious, diabolical death-wave! Yes, somewhere in the heavens, upon some one of those brilliant, beautiful planets, gleaming like jewels in the velvet sky above my head, sentient, living, intelligent and horribly inhuman beings must even now be watching us, plotting to destroy us, sending those death-dealing, invisible waves through space. But, thanks to Henderson, we had conquered those. Yes, rendered them harmless.

I stopped in my walk, looked up at the brilliant stars and shook my fist at them savagely. "Yes, by Heaven!" I cried, "we've beaten you at that game, and we'll beat you at the other!"

Just below Mars a tiny point of light appeared in the sky. Like a distant airplane it moved slowly across the heavens. Swiftly it increased in size. The heavens seemed to pale. In a brilliant, dazzling flash it vanished beyond the distant horizon.

I laughed hoarsely. "All right, you damnable beasts!" I exclaimed. "Send them down! Do your worst! But our turn will come."

The only answer was a dull, far-distant detonation, the muffled explosion of the falling missile, as we believed it to be.

By the next morning more than twenty meteors had fallen upon the harassed world—more than during any previous twenty-four hours. And nine had struck cities and towns. The average of hits was still being sustained. Fortunately, however, no really important nor very large cities had been destroyed. However, northwestern Pennsylvania had been laid waste. As I read the news, I wondered when New York would fall, when Boston would be leveled, when London would be wiped out. My thoughts were interrupted by the telephone ringing. Henderson's voice greeted me.

"Good news!" he exclaimed jubilantly. "Come on over. I think I've got it."

Needless to say I lost little time in reaching his home, a remodeled farm in Westchester.

"I suppose you've read the papers," he exclaimed as he greeted me. "Twenty-three of 'em in the last twenty-four hours, and nine bull's eyes! But it's an ill wind, etc., you know. I'll bet you couldn't guess where I spent the night. After you left I did a lot of figuring along the lines you suggested—I'm glad you were here and thought of it—and then I went over to see old Fothergill. He's an astronomer you know, not a scientist…" He laughed slightly. "…just an amateur. Astronomy's his pet hobby—rich as the devil and spends fortunes on his fad. He's the fellow who writes on 'Housetop Astronomy.' You know…he also runs that column in the *News*, 'Stars of the Month.' Signs himself, 'Aries.' He's a sensible chap and I told him my idea and that I wanted to use his telescope—with his help of course—and we spent the whole night watching for meteors. We spotted seventeen, and watched eleven—couldn't follow all at once, you see.

Merritt, every one of the eleven came from the same spot and followed exactly the same course! And the place where they first came into sight, and the course they followed tallied exactly with all my calculations!"

"Fine!" I exclaimed. "Did you come to any conclusions as to where they originated? Was there any planet at the place where they appeared?"

Henderson grinned. "No, of course not," he replied. "We didn't expect there would be. We—"

"Great Scott, man, I thought you *did* expect they came from some planet!" I cried.

"Sure," he declared, "but the things don't come straight any more than a bullet shot from a long distance. They come from the devil of a distance and have to be aimed way ahead of our old world in order to hit it. And of course they're not visible until they're pretty close to us within our atmosphere. Even a thousand-ton meteor is a mighty small thing to see a few miles away. So you see, old man, when we catch sight of them, they're on the last lap of their journey and the final curve of their trajectory, and—the place they come from would be way off to one side—might be out of sight on the other side of the world in fact."

"Then how on earth are you going to find out where they come from or if they come from anywhere?" I demanded.

"I'm afraid *I* couldn't," admitted Henderson. "But that's where old Fothergill came in. He's steeped to the neck in astronomy, and is a wizard at higher mathematics. Calculating parabolas is his greatest stunt, and he's a regular wizard at it. Why, if Fothergill should see a snake wiggle ten feet, I'll bet he could calculate every wiggle it had made in traveling for half a mile back. He sent me his calculations just before I telephoned you, and according to him the curves of every one of those eleven meteors, if traced back through space, lead slap-bang to Mars!"

"By Jove!" I exclaimed. "Then you think—it's certain they are hurled at us from Mars!"

"I'm sure of it," he declared. "But to make assurance doubly sure, I've given Fothergill all my figures and data on the past meteor falls. He's going to go over them, check them up, and try to work out the curves and see if they agree with last night's. Then we'll be dead certain."

When Fothergill's results arrived shortly after noon, there was absolutely no doubt of it. Even with the casual observations of the other astronomers who had recorded the meager statistics regarding the meteors, the millionaire amateur astronomer had proved conclusively that in every case, the meteorites had come from practically the same location in the heavens. In every case that point coincided almost precisely with the position of Mars. But Fothergill had gone even farther. He assured Henderson—in whose theory he had now become intensely interested—that with the knowledge they had thus obtained, it would be quite possible to forecast the locality where meteorites might be expected to strike on any given date.

"That," I declared, "is the most important thing yet, Henderson. If you and Fothergill can warn the public beforehand it will save thousands of lives, even if it does not prevent property losses."

"But none will believe it," he replied. "Even if the public has faith in such prophecies, the scientists and officials will pooh-pooh them."

"The only way to be sure of that is to try it and see," I said. "I admit that in the beginning no one would have listened to such theories, but after making your other discoveries and proving them to everybody's satisfaction, I think they'll have faith in you now. Besides, you've got Fothergill to back you up. Even if he's an amateur, as you call it, his knowledge of astronomy and mathematics is acknowledged by the most eminent scientists. They can't scoff at him or his hard and fast facts."

The next day Henderson gave the result of his observations and deductions to the world through the medium of the *Times* and other papers. But as he had feared (and as I had not foreseen) with little result. To be sure, a large portion of the public eagerly accepted his theories and proofs; but a larger portion scoffed at them.

Once again the press and the public entered into a controversy for and against the Henderson theory. Those in his favor demanded that steps should be taken to protect life by following Henderson's suggestions; those on the other side insisted that it was all utter nonsense, that even while they admitted that he had benefited mankind beyond estimation by his former discovery, he had overreached himself by suggesting such a wild and untenable theory as the present one. Some even hinted that the affair had affected his brain, while one prominent daily took a humorous attitude and suggested that if Henderson could now foretell where a meteorite would strike, he should go a step farther and inform the public how they could be prevented from striking.

"The one would be as sensible as the other," the writer concluded. "If it were not so serious it would be farcical," declared another paper. "Even in these days there are limits to human credulity. We do not desire to belittle Lord—or is it *Professor*—Henderson's intelligence and attainments, nor do we overlook or underestimate what he has given to the world already; but this time we feel sure his imagination has got the better of his common sense.

"All astronomers and scientists, to whom we have submitted the matter agree that it would be utterly impossible for inhabitants (admitting there *are* inhabitants) of Mars or any other planet to project meteoric or other masses of metal through space so that they would strike Earth. It would be, they state, like attempting to hit a six-inch shell with a rifle at a distance of several thousand yards from the projectile. Even assuming that if countless hundreds of thousands of objects were discharged from Mars in the hopes that a few might by chance strike Earth, it would be still more impossible to direct any of these so accurately as to intentionally strike a city. It would be beyond the capabilities of any intelligence to compute the frictional resistance of our atmosphere, the wind currents, and the thousand and one other local factors that would affect the passage of a meteor falling through our atmospheric envelope.

"Regarding the mathematical data that have been submitted in proof of the theory, we have been assured by several of the most eminent mathematicians that almost any theory may be mathematically proven if the mathematician assumes a certain factor and works backward from that factor. The whole thing is interesting, entertaining, and would form a most excellent plot for a work of fiction. It outdoes Jules Verne and Wells, but as fact we cannot accept it.

"If Doctor—or is it *Chevalier*—Henderson and his associate, Mr. Richard Fothergill, feel so confident of their 'discovery,' we would suggest that they go a step farther and prove their claims by giving a forecast of the coming meteors—a prophecy as to the cities that are doomed by the Martians—to be destroyed during the next few days."

To my surprise, such scurrilous articles, downright insulting comments, criticisms, and accusations (not to mention the disbelief and ridicule) that Henderson's announcement aroused did not appear to cause him pain. On the contrary, they aroused his anger, his resentment, and his scorn; and old Fothergill fairly raged. He had been completely won over to Henderson's ideas; he had proved to his own satisfaction that Henderson was right, and he had enthusiastically devoted all his knowledge, his time, and his intelligence to the matter.

"Fools! Idiots! Consummate asses!" he cried, his gray hair and beard fairly bristling. "Anything they cannot understand is impossible. Impossible, *hah!* The only impossible thing in the universe is to find common sense in the average human being! Intelligence? *Hah!* Fiddlesticks! They haven't any. They're still running about as purposeless as ants in a dunghill. I'm not sure—no, I'm not by any means sure that they deserve being saved from their own stupidity. I'm not by any means certain that the world would not be better off without them. I'm not positive that I'm not in thorough sympathy with the Martians. If they can observe us—as they probably can—I can scarcely blame them for endeavoring to annihilate us."

"I won't put it quite as strong as that," said Henderson. "I'm as thoroughly disgusted as you are, but I expected it. But it's not so much the fault of the people and their intellect as it is human self-conceit. Human beings have lorded it over nature—upon Earth—for so long that they have acquired the fixed impression that they are literally 'Lords of Creation.' They are puffed up—even if unconsciously—with their own importance. They feel that the whole universe is centered here on Earth; that they are the most intelligent, most important beings in the universe.

"They have taken to themselves the monopoly of being immortal, of having souls. They have even had the effrontery to picture God as a glorified *man*. Sublime in their egoism, they cannot conceive of any being equal or superior to them; they cannot imagine any intelligent beings that are not patterned on the same general lines as human beings. In fact, few can really conceive of sentient intelligent beings that are not men and women, and not inhabitants of this planet.

"In the minds of nine hundred and ninety-nine persons out of every thousand, only one being in the entire universe is greater than mankind, and that is God Himself. They are quite ready to believe that God Almighty has seen fit to hurl these meteors at Earth, but they are not willing to admit that any other mortals are more intelligent, more powerful than themselves. That's the whole trouble, Fothergill.

"But we've got to convince them. If you saw a man trying to jump into the river, you'd grab him if you could and try to prevent him from taking his own life, even if he was a worthless good-for-nothing bum. And I look at the human race as a lot of addle-headed, hide-bound fools, most of whom are to all intents and purposes trying their best to commit suicide."

"And how, may I ask, are you going to stop them?" demanded Fothergill.

"How would you stop the bum from jumping into the river as soon as your back was turned?" laughed Henderson. "By convincing him of the truth of your arguments that he was wrong and you were right, of course. Well, that's just how I'm going to reduce the number of self-sacrifices among the masses."

"I'm afraid you'll have a hard time doing it," I observed. "And even with your knowledge—even though you, Fothergill, myself, and thousands of others are convinced that these damnable things *are* being shot at us from Mars, I cannot see that, as yet, you have evolved any scheme for stopping them."

"No, I admit I haven't—yet," he replied. "But if I could convince the disbelievers that we can foretell the danger areas on certain dates, we could save a lot of lives as you yourself said."

"Then for Heaven's sake why haven't you done it?" I asked. "If you had published a warning and it had been borne out, the public would be forced to believe."

"For two reasons," replied Henderson. "In the first place, Fothergill and I wanted to be absolutely dead certain we could forecast accurately. And in the second place we were a little afraid of creating a panic. There are a lot of nervous people who would go crazy if they had faith in our forecasts and believed their homes were doomed to be smashed within the next day or two."

"But no longer," he continued rather savagely. "We've convinced ourselves we can prophesy pretty accurately—we both agreed that last night's fall would concentrate on northeastern Canada and it did—Quebec, Halifax and part of Montreal went; and it's better to frighten a few hundred people to death or to drive them insane than to have thousands killed. We've pretty well worked out the probabilities of tomorrow's bombardment, and I'm going to publish it today."

I gasped. "Then you really can—you, you think? For God's sake, Henderson, tell me—what's going to happen tomorrow—what city is going to be hit?"

He smiled. "You see how excited *you* get over it," he replied. "And you're not a nervous man. You can imagine what the effect will be upon others—particularly women. But I'm convinced we've got to use the homeopathic principle. If our calculations are not at fault, you'll see by the Thursday papers that several of England's most important cities have ceased to exist..."

When the papers appeared containing Henderson's statement that the meteorites falling on Wednesday would be concentrated on the British Isles, and that Manchester, Sheffield; Leeds, Carlisle or other Midland and northern cities would probably be hit, the effect was manifold.

Some scoffed at the prophecy, made fun of it, regarded it as a joke or a hoax. Sporting people laid wagers on it. One paper, in an editorial, sarcastically thanked Henderson for being so considerate as to divert his Martian projectiles from the United States to England, and remarked that it was a great pity he had not made his "discovery" at the time of the World War, as in that case he might have induced his Martian friends to devote their attentions to Germany. Many were loud in their denunciations, declaring that Henderson was a scare-head, that if he were permitted to continue he would have the entire world in a state of hysterical fear, and that he should be restrained, or the papers forbidden to publish such news.

In England the feeling appeared to be divided between resentment that Henderson should have selected the British as the next to suffer, and self-satisfied confidence that it was all "bally nonsense." There was no fear, no panic, no nervousness. The race that had gone calmly on with its daily tasks despite Zeppelin and airplane raids was not one to be terrified because some "crank" overseas had warned them of an impending shower of meteors.

Nevertheless, a goodly portion of the inhabitants of the cities named decided that there might be something in it, and in motor cars, trams, chars-a-bancs, trains, buses and afoot, sought the open spaces and small villages. And the insurance companies blessed the name of Henderson. The British may be conservative, they may not be easily scared, but they are a thrifty, cautious people—more especially in the north—and they are probably the most insured and assured people on Earth. So whether or not they had faith in Henderson's forecast, the inhabitants of the district he had mentioned lost no time in taking out new and larger policies on property and life.

I do not, of course, know how the public at large felt, as the time drew near for the fulfillment of Henderson's prophecy. But I do know that I was keyed up, excited, and nervous. I was torn between doubts and fears. As far as I was personally concerned, it made really little, if any, difference to me whether or not England's manufacturing centers and midland cities were or were not destroyed. Of course it would be a lamentable and unfortunate thing if they were, but I—and the world—had become so accustomed to cities being wiped out, that such disasters had, to a large extent, lost their horror. And although it may have peen most selfish and inhumane—not to say unchristian—our feeling, when we heard of a city being struck elsewhere, was largely one of thankfulness that it had not been our own.

But it is one thing to know that, nine times out of ten, the morning news would tell us of a disaster somewhere, and quite another thing to have the disaster promised, and to be awaiting it.

I wondered how the inhabitants of the supposedly doomed cities were taking it. I wondered what the effect would be if they escaped; what would be the result if Henderson's forecast was fulfilled. And I wondered how many lives he would have saved if it was fulfilled. Yet, so confident was I that Henderson and Fothergill were right; so firmly did I now believe in Henderson's theory of the Martian origin of the meteors, that I was as sure that the Thursday morning papers would tell of the disaster as I was that the sun would rise on that same morning. And yet, when I glanced at the front page and saw the news staring me in the face, I could scarcely believe my eyes.

Henderson had been right. His prophecy had been fulfilled! Sheffield, Kendall, a part of Leeds, and Sunderland had been reduced to smoking ruins; several smaller towns had been utterly destroyed, and near five thousand lives had been lost. But, thanks to Henderson's warning—and the stalwart British press unanimously gave him full credit for this—many more thousands had been saved from death.

Henderson's triumph was complete. Once more he had convinced the world he had been right. Criticism, ridicule, sarcasm, disbelief were transformed to praise, plaudits, honors, almost adoration. He was hailed as the greatest genius of the world, the hero of the hour, the man to whom the world looks for its salvation.

CHAPTER SEVEN

The World is Saved

BEING the most prominent and popular man in the world has its drawbacks. Henderson was deluged with telegrams, radio messages and cablegrams. He was swamped with letters. He was besieged by reporters, callers and cranks. His home was surrounded by crowds gazing, staring, curious, seeming to find immense satisfaction in merely seeing where he lived. And of course Fothergill came in for his share of attention. His name had been linked with Henderson's, and Henderson insisted that what had been accomplished was due more to Fothergill than to himself. But the public, remembering what he had done before, was all for Henderson.

By far the greater portion of the cables and radiograms came from England. Some were from the editors of the London dailies and weeklies offering fabulous sums for articles on his newest theories and discoveries, or for forecasts to be published daily. Others were from officials expressing the Britishers' appreciation of Henderson's services in preventing greater loss of life, and he even received a message from Buckingham Palace assuring him in formal terms of the gratitude of the British Empire as represented by His Majesty the King. But by far the greater part of the flood of communications were pleas for Henderson to evolve some means of putting an end to the destruction by the Martian projectiles.

Many of these offered Henderson unlimited powers and unlimited resources for carrying on the necessary experiments and investigations. The President called a special session of Congress to put through a bill for the purpose of providing funds for the purpose; but before our government had its rather ponderous machinery in operation, the British had acted, and had placed all of England's resources at Henderson's disposal. And, before the day was done, practically every government had assured Henderson of unstinted cooperation if he would devote himself to trying to devise a means of saving the world from its impending fate. Also, every government had besought Henderson and Fothergill to continue sending out their forecasts in order that the doomed districts might be evacuated, and the lives of their inhabitants thus saved.

But Fothergill was not yet appeased by any means. The way in which the public had received his and Henderson's announcement a few days previously still rankled in his mind. "We don't want their money," he declared. "Let them keep it. They'll need it all before they're through, before they rebuild their cities. And they'll have to keep on rebuilding—as fast as they build, they'll be knocked over like toy blocks, if human beings are going to exist, they'll have to burrow into the earth. Stop the things! Good Lord…do the fools think any power on Earth can stop them?

"That's human nature for you; one minute denying the possibility of the real, the next asking for the impossible. But I'm willing to do all we can. I'm ready and willing—only too glad—to collaborate with Henderson and work out forecasts for weeks ahead. But not a cent of public or private money will be used. I'm in this. I've always wanted to expend some of my money for the benefit of the world, and now I have the chance. Whatever is done will be done with my money. You can tell the world that, Henderson."

I smiled. "But, my dear Mr. Fothergill," I expostulated, "your money—even your millions, are limited. Suppose—just suppose for a moment—that you or Henderson should evolve a theory as to how to prevent the attacks, or if not to prevent them, how to mitigate them. It would cost an enormous amount to provide the world with devices or apparatus or whatever it might be to carry your discovery into effect. No single fortune could pay for it. Why think what it must have cost to provide the public with Henderson's protective suits and resuscitating devices. What then? Wouldn't you be willing to accept outside funds?"

"Humph, that's a different matter," he declared, a twinkle in his eyes. "Yes, once we make a discovery—and prove it—I'm willing that the public or individuals should finance it to completion."

"Bother the financial end of it," burst in Henderson. "We're getting nowhere. The first thing to be done is to work out the courses of the damned things for a long time ahead, and then see if we can't think up some way of getting the best of the Martians."

Fothergill sniffed. "The first portion of your remarks I concur with fully," he said. "But even that master mind of yours, Paul—your marvelous imagination and your almost uncanny abilities—will never, I am relatively certain, be able to cope successfully with the super-intellects that are directing these projectiles from Mars. So I suggest that we eliminate any such ideas from our minds for the present time and leave our brains free to work out the involved calculations that are of paramount importance."

As the result of the calculations, the newspapers throughout the world on the following day published a forecast for the succeeding week. And as the world read, it stood aghast. Never before had the public fully realized what the bombardment from the heavens really meant. But now, as they read the prophecies, as they saw city after city doomed to swift destruction, as they read the cold print telling them that their own homes would almost certainly come tumbling to ruins on a certain day, the horror, the awfulness of the relentless destruction was brought home to them.

People opened their papers with fear and trembling, dreading to see the name of their own city on the list, hoping against hope that it would not appear, and yet realizing that, in its very appearance, they were being saved from probable death. And, aside from saving countless lives, the forecasts saved millions, billions of dollars' worth of property. The governments took charge and whenever a city's probable destruction was forecast, every effort was made to remove everything of great or irreplaceable value from the city. All records, archives, art treasures and public property were kept in constant readiness to be moved at a moment's notice, and every citizen was warned to be in readiness to move, bag and baggage, the instant his city was included in the prophecy.

At first, of course, little was salvaged in this way. The forecasts covered only a few days or a week at most in advance. But as Henderson and Fothergill labored incessantly and grudgingly, employed a large corps of trained scientists and mathematicians as assistants, they were able to extend their forecasts, and within a few weeks the papers were publishing the names of cities and the districts to be devastated two or three months in advance. Hence there was ample time to move all the most important valuables to areas beyond the spheres of destruction.

When Boston was reduced to ruins, the remains were those of empty, deserted shells. When west London was shattered, the Tate Gallery, the Houses of Parliament, the Chelsea Hospital, Westminster Abbey, Buckingham Palace, and every other public building in the area had been vacated for weeks before.

Of course the loss of edifices, the destruction of historical buildings and monuments, the losses to business and industry were irreparable and beyond estimate. But the loss of life, documents, records, valuables, was almost negligible. Moreover, there was time to erect temporary housings for the people, vaults for the funds, libraries, and other buildings. And as it was soon evident that the new cities and towns that sprang up were very rarely included in the forecasts, people began to breathe more freely.

To Henderson this rather amazing and seemingly chance feature of the affair was most interesting. He declared that it was most important, and after several weeks of silence, came out with a new announcement. The Martians, he declared, could not, as had been thought, watch Earth. At any rate they could not distinguish the details such as cities and towns. By some unknown means they had maps—or plans of Earth, they had known the approximate location of every large city, every important town, even the most important and regular steamship lanes. They had hurled their projectiles with almost supernatural accuracy at these—much, as he put it, as a modern artilleryman aims his huge gun at an invisible target by means of a plotted map.

But that they could not actually see the cities was, he insisted, proved by the fact that only two out of the hundreds of new cities had been struck, and these two had been so near other older cities that it was probable they had been hit by accident and not by design. Herein, he stated, lay the safety—at least for the present—of civilization. Build new cities at safe distances from the former centers, and until the Martians had, by some occult means, discovered their locations, they would be practically safe.

No doubt, he continued, Earth's planetary enemies took it for granted that their projectiles were fulfilling all expectations. They probably assumed that human beings could not escape the death-waves, that their intelligence was not sufficiently developed to enable them to escape entire destruction, and hence the Martians would not dream that the population of Earth had been comparatively unaffected, and that new centers of industry, life and civilization were being erected to replace those destroyed.

His announcement met with the heartiest response and a universal approval. The whole world had completely altered in its attitude towards Henderson. Had he announced that the meteorites were living, thinking beings from another planet, the public, I verily believe, would have agreed with him.

Still the meteorites, or projectiles—as I must learn to call them—continued to fall. They neither increased nor decreased in numbers, but fell in more or less intermittent showers—sometimes two or three, sometimes fifteen or twenty every twenty-four hours—and the percentage of their hits remained very nearly constant. That, Henderson argued, was still further proof that the Martians could not observe the effects of their shots. If they could they would have improved in their accuracy. They would have corrected their trajectories, and through the months that had passed, the percentage of hits would have greatly increased.

And then came his greatest, most epochal discovery. The meteorites—projectiles I should say—still lay wherever they had fallen. The earlier ones had, of course, dwindled in size through their loss by the constantly emanating death-waves. But every one was a constant source of danger. To venture within the area of their waves without being equipped with the wave-proof outfits meant death, and it was neither practical nor possible for human beings to constantly wear these cumbersome suits.

Moreover, since Henderson's and Fothergill's forecasts had become universally accepted and proved, there had been no occasion to wear the garments. And while the public had learned to give the things a wide berth, and barriers had been erected carrying warnings about every projectile, still they were a danger and a great nuisance. There were so many of them, and in some districts they were so near together, that the arable lands and available city sites were greatly restricted. And as time went on there would be more and more of them accumulating.

Hence Henderson devoted a vast amount of time to experimenting with ideas and devices designed to render the projectiles harmless. So if, he reasoned, his resuscitating apparatus rearranged the disorganized atoms of the human brain and thus offset the action of the death-waves, would not some form of wave nullify the undulatory emanations before they were given off by the projectiles? In other words, was it not possible to utilize some form of wave to alter the atomic or electronic arrangement of the projectiles themselves, and by so doing render them partially or completely incapable of receiving and transmitting the unknown, mysterious waves that, he still believed, were coming through space from Mars?

He was convinced that this was possible, and with his samples of the projectiles, he set patiently, doggedly to work along these lines of reasoning.

So when my phone rang one afternoon and I heard Henderson's excited and jubilant voice at the other end of the wire, I knew he had made an important discovery of some sort.

"Come over just as soon as you can!" he cried. "It's wonderful! Absolutely astounding! I want you to be the first to see it."

"What's astounding?" I asked. "Have you found what you were looking for?"

"No," he yelled, "but something a lot better. Come on!"

I found him even more excited and enthusiastic than I had judged from his voice. He was fairly aglow with enthusiasm.

"Now put on this wave-proof suit," he cried. "I'm going to show you something that'll make your eyes pop out."

As he spoke he was donning another of his suits, and wondering what on earth it was all about, I obeyed his instructions. Then he led me to his laboratory.

"See that?" he cried, pointing to a lump of black mineral that I recognized as a fragment of one of the meteorites—projectiles rather.

I nodded.

"Well just watch it," he cried.

As he spoke, he began arranging a complicated-looking device of wires, magnets and small vacuum tubes upon the bench.

"Now!" he exclaimed. "Keep your eyes on it. Ready? One…two…three…!" As he uttered the word "three" he pressed a switch, and as if shot from a gun, the fragment of mineral leaped from the table and struck with a resounding thud against the ceiling where it remained. I stared, mouth gaping, at the thing. What the devil had shot it into the air! Why did it stay there as if fastened to the ceiling?

Henderson laughed. "I thought I'd surprise you," he declared. "Now watch. I press this switch and…"

I heard a click as he moved the switch and instantly the bit of metal tumbled back to the table.

"Well I'll be…" I began.

"No you won't," he chuckled, interrupting me. "But I don't blame you for being flabbergasted. I was myself."

"But, what does it all mean? How's it done?" I demanded.

"It means the salvation of the world," said Henderson calmly and very seriously, "and it's done by means of a very simple high-frequency current of electricity in combination with a vibratory wave of a certain length. You see," he went on, "I've been experimenting, as you know, with devices to nullify the death-waves from these things. I tried every darned thing—every form of current and wave and ray I could think of, and with no success.

"Just this morning I had a high-frequency current apparatus here, and a little specially designed transmitting set. I was sitting here thinking, wondering, staring at that lump of Martian devilishness, and unconsciously letting my fingers monkey with the instruments. Suddenly and without any warning, the darned thing flew past my head and slammed against the ceiling and stuck there. I couldn't believe my eyes, couldn't imagine what had happened. Then I began to reason. Either it was some outside influence—some ray or wave of something from Mars—or else it was something in here that had caused the thing to act as it had. The other specimens hadn't moved, so I decided it must be due to something in here. The only things I had touched or moved were the generator and transmitter, so I reasoned it must have some type of connection with them. I examined them and—well, believe it or not—I found I had swung two switches and had turned on the current from the generator and had set the transmitter going at the same time. It seemed impossible, but I couldn't account for it in any other way. So I kept my eye on the lump and moved the switches back...*Plump!*

"Down came the thing to the table again. I swung the switches back and...*Bang!*

"Up she goes to the ceiling. Then I rang you. It won't work with either of the switches alone. Both have to be swung together. Now I know how the darned thing works and the rest is simple. Merritt!" he cried. "If I'm not crazy, the world's as good as saved."

"If you can explain how you think it's saved, I can judge better," I told him. "I may be awfully dense, but I fail to see how this trick of popping the bit of mineral up and down—remarkable as it is—can save the world."

"Yes, I must admit it. You *are* dense," laughed Henderson. "Now let me explain. Why does this lump of metal jump up in the air when I use the high-frequency current and the short radio wave? Because, my dear boy, there's something about the stuff that causes it to be violently repelled by that particular combination of a wave and a high-frequency current.

"There are two hypothetical explanations for that. There may be some intrinsic property of the stuff that causes it to be repelled. But I doubt that. On the other hand, we know—at least I feel sure—that the death-waves are actuated by some other form of waves coming from Mars. In other words there is a direct radio connection or communication established between Mars and these projectiles here on Earth.

"We know—everyone familiar with electricity and radio knows—that certain waves may be nullified or obliterated or even completely altered by the impingement of other waves. Very well, assuming that there are waves connecting Mars with every one of these masses—with every fragment, and assuming that the combined wave and current I have here strikes that Martian wave, what happens? Why, up flies the bit of Martian metal until it plunks into the ceiling and has to stop. But does it fall back? Not a bit of it. There it sticks despite all the laws of gravity, until I shut off my magic and back it comes.

"In other words, and to relieve the strain on your mentality, old man, I've nullified or altered or annihilated the wave that connects Mars and this precious little lump of cussedness, and so there's nothing for the dear thing to do, but run home and tell mother up in Mars. But as there's a ceiling in the way, it can't go home and just sticks as far up as it can go."

"You mean…" I exclaimed, trying my best to understand just what he did mean and overlooking his flippancy, "…you mean that the only thing that holds the meteorites—or whatever they are—on Earth, is the wave or ray or whatever it is that connects them with Mars, and that when it is shut off they fly back to the place they came from?"

"I can't say that is *exactly* my theory," he replied. "I'm not quite prepared as yet to scrap the idea of gravity, or that solid metal will not remain on Earth without outside help. No, what I believe is, that the waves connecting these things with Mars are the same waves, or a portion of the same waves, that were used to send them here and to direct them. And I believe—in fact I am sure—that my little dinkus here produces a combination that reverses the Martian waves and causes them to attract just as powerfully as they repelled. If that—"

"Lord!" I shouted in my excitement. "Then you think that with proper devices you can cause these—these projectiles, to leave Earth and hurl themselves back to Mars?"

"Precisely," he declared. "Now you see, Merritt, what I meant when I said the world was as good as saved."

I got up and paced the floor, my mind in a turmoil, striving to think the thing out, to find flaws in what seemed an incredible and yet such a reasonable theory. It was too big to be grasped at once. The idea of an electric current and a radio wave being able to lift those enormous masses and project them through space was beyond belief. I turned to Henderson, who was amusing himself by shooting the bit of mineral into the air and letting it drop back.

"But, Paul," I demanded, "how do you know it will work on a big mass of the stuff? Don't a lot of experiments work on a small scale and fail in a big test? And—well, somehow I can't believe a wave, electricity, can have the power to move such things. Why, man, it would take more gunpowder than there is in existence even to fire one of the darned things a few hundred yards."

Henderson roared with laughter. "All for the big noise and the flash and smoke!" he cried. "Do you doubt the power of electricity when an electric locomotive hauls your train at seventy miles an hour? Do you question the power of electricity when you see huge factories, mills, all operating on the same invisible thing? If an electric crane with an electromagnet can lift a hundred ton casting, is there any reason why an electric current should not lift one thousand tons? And if a radio wave can transmit your words and your picture around the world, is there any reason why it should not do things no more remarkable in their way, even if they are new?"

"No, I don't suppose there is," I admitted. "But," I added, "I'm still a bit of a doubting Thomas, and I'd like to see one of those thousand—or even hundred-ton meteorites go sky-shooting off into space, just because you turn a switch near it."

"That, my dear friend, is just what you shall see," he assured me. "As soon as I can rig up a large enough apparatus, I'm going to make the test. Now don't say a thing about this. Keep it mum until we *know.* I'm not going to be laughed at again, and I'm not going to get the whole world in a state of expectation and then disappoint it. I haven't even told Fothergill yet, but just as soon as I'm ready, I'll invite you both to the test, and if I'm not terribly mistaken, we'll have the supreme satisfaction of seeing some of these unwelcome visitors go tearing back to their senders."

I chuckled. "In that case," I said, "I wonder what the Martians will think when the things come shooting back to them."

"Yes, I wonder," he said. "But I'll guarantee that if it works out as I expect and hope it will, the Martians won't enjoy it. They'll be getting a taste of their own medicine. I wonder if they've got any big cities to be knocked to pieces. Too bad we can't watch the results."

I could hardly contain myself for the next few days. I dreamed nightly of Henderson's latest discovery. I had nightmares about it. It filled every moment of my days. And when less than a week later he called me and informed me—in quite casual tones—that all was ready for the test, I felt as nervous and excited as though I personally were about to start on a journey through space.

I found Henderson awaiting me with Fothergill. The latter seemed to take the affair quite as a matter of course, and as we climbed into Henderson's car he spoke quite casually of it.

"I've another item that will interest you," Henderson informed me. "Fothergill has calculated the length of time it should take for the things to get back to Mars, and he believes that it may be possible for observers on Earth to note the effect of the things when they hit."

"*If* they hit…" I reminded him.

"Oh, I'm confident they will," he replied. "If we can start 'em off they'll go home to roost all right."

Our first objective was a meteorite—no, projectile—about fifty miles from town. It was one that had fallen several months previously, one of the same shower that had destroyed Schenectady and Poughkeepsie and had caused tremendous damages to Albany, Northampton and Saratoga. It lay in an uninhabited district and was particularly well suited to Henderson's experiment.

"Besides, there are two or three others not far away," he said, as we raced along the Hudson Boulevard. "If we fail on one we'll try another, and if one works, we'll start all of them on their way."

Reaching the vicinity of the projectile, Henderson turned into an abandoned road, once an important state highway but now overgrown, out of repair, and never used on account of its proximity to the thing we sought. A mile farther on we came to a barbed-wire fence bearing the usual government warning of a meteorite.

Here Henderson stopped his car, brought out the wave-proof suits we were to wear, and unloaded several heavy and cumbersome, cases.

"Too bad we couldn't get nearer the thing," he grunted as he lifted some instrument from the car. "And too bad we couldn't bring along some husky fellows to carry these things. But we'll manage somehow. There's plenty of time and we can take one at a time if necessary."

I admit that it was hard work getting the things up to the meteorite, but we accomplished it at last. I had never been so near one of the things before, and I looked at it curiously. It was three-quarters buried in the earth, a harmless-looking, blackish, slightly rusty mass that might have been a huge boulder. But, for several hundred yards about it, every vestige of vegetation had been completely wiped out. Remains of charred trees and piles of ashes covered the up-thrown earth that was burned a vivid brick-red, and for nearly a mile in every direction the trees had died and stood gaunt—pathetic testimonials to the heat of the thing when it fell.

"How close to the darned thing shall I put this box?" I asked Henderson.

He scratched his head and grinned. "Hanged if I know," he admitted. "We don't want to get too near. When that baby wakes up and starts for home, he's going to kick up a lot of dust and dirt and raise the devil about here. I've tried out the things in my laboratory, and if the big ones work on the same principle and in the same ratio, then we ought to be able to give it a kick from about fifty yards off. But I'll make it surer and say thirty yards. That's safe enough. Don't you think so, Fothergill?"

"Hmmm, I should imagine so," he assented. "Aside from the dust and dirt it throws off, I cannot see that there is any danger to be apprehended. If your theory is correct—as I have no doubt it is—it will be drawn, not projected from here. In that case there should be no concussion, no recoil. It should leave its bed smoothly and silently. I think even ten yards would be quite safe."

"We'll split the difference and say twenty, then," said Henderson, grinning. "All right, let's hook her up and say goodbye."

Very quickly the boxes were unpacked, the various instruments assembled, and the innumerable connections and wires properly arranged by Henderson. Fothergill and myself could do nothing to help. The apparatus was all Greek to us. But as we watched, it seemed too utterly preposterous to think that the little instruments Henderson was fussing over, those mahogany and bake-lite cabinets and panels with their nickel knobs and connections and green-coated wires could even affect, much less move that huge, dull, rusty mass of metal lying firmly in the soil.

"All Okay!" Henderson said at last, straightening up. "Now, ladies and gentlemen..." He laughed. "...we are about to demonstrate to you the truth of the old saying that faith can move mountains. Keep your eyes on yonder sullen mass of mineral, my friends, and see if you can tell how the trick is done; see if the eye is faster than the hand, as the conjurers say. All ready? Hold hard! One, two—"

There was a sharp click, a deafening roar. I was lifted from my feet, whirled mightily about, spun like a top and then thrown flat on my face. Confused, gasping, scared, and the breath knocked from my lungs, I sat up and stared about. A few feet away Fothergill was blinking his eyes, spitting dirt from his mouth, and rubbing his shoulder. Off to the other side Henderson was slowly rising to his feet and gazing in a half-dazed manner towards the meteorite. I turned and stared in the same direction.

The next instant I leaped to my feet and let out a yell like a Comanche. The thing had vanished! Where it had rested a moment before was only a shallow pit into which dirt and pebbles were slowly sliding. I could not believe my eyes. Then, as I gazed at the spot, I was aware of a peculiar greenish light that seemed to flood everything.

Henderson's voice brought me to my senses.

"Hurrah!" he yelled, "it worked! Number one's off on its way!"

"But what the deuce happened?" I asked, still confused and a bit breathless.

"I hadn't thought of that," Henderson replied somewhat slowly. "It's a good thing that we weren't any nearer. Between the outrush of displaced air in front and the inrush to fill the vacuum behind the thing, we got pretty well knocked about. And, say, notice the green light? I hadn't thought of that either. That old boy certainly *is* traveling. Too bad it isn't dark so we could watch it go."

He stepped towards his instruments and bent forward. Fothergill leaped upon him with a sharp cry and flung him back.

"For God's sake, don't touch it!" he yelled. "Do you want that blazing thing to come hurtling back here?"

CHAPTER EIGHT
What Happened to Mars

"WHEW!" exclaimed Henderson. "I *did* come near putting my foot in it that time! Thanks for stopping me, Fothergill. I completely forgot about that. Funny how I could. Well, that puts the kibosh on sending off any more of the darned things."

"What's it all about?" I queried. "What did you come near putting your foot in, Henderson? What did you forget, and why isn't it possible to start more meteors—or projectiles—on their homeward journey?"

The others laughed heartily. "Don't you understand?" cried Henderson. "If I switch off the confounded thing that mass of molten metal—it's molten by this time right enough—will turn around and come galumping back here. I've got to keep the switch on until the thing hits Mars!"

"And, possibly, even then it might return," put in Fothergill, "that's a matter we—or rather you, Paul—hadn't thought of."

Henderson grinned. "Sort of rubber ball effect," he remarked. " 'Twould be funny if the things were to go bounding back and forth between here and Mars. But I don't think there's any danger of that. Once they get home I'll bet they stay there—unless the Martians fire 'em back again. And I don't believe that one would come back even if I shut the current off. I'm going to try it."

"Hold on," I warned him. "I don't want to be here when it comes back."

"No danger to us," declared Fothergill. "If it returned now, it wouldn't strike here. Earth has moved a good many miles since it left. But you could not feel certain one way or the other if you did switch off the current, Paul. Even if it returned you could not distinguish it from a new body."

"Hmmm, that's so," admitted Henderson, then he said with a laugh, "Looks as though I'll have to tag them when I send them off, so as to be able to identify them."

"I think," said Fothergill judicially, "that by operating at night we may be able to determine if it is essential to keep your apparatus in action in order to prevent their return. We could then watch the—er—objects until they were barely visible. Then, if you switched off your device and they continued to recede, we could be quite sure that they would *not* return."

"Fine," replied Henderson. "I'll switch this off any how. If the thing comes back it won't make any great difference—one more or less is of no consequence nowadays. And tonight we'll try the stunt."

I confess that as Henderson shut off the current I had a feeling of apprehension, and ridiculous as it was, I couldn't help glancing up, half-expecting to see the huge mass of incandescent metal come hurtling back at us. But nothing happened. I might have realized that nothing would, for at the tremendous speed at which it was traveling, it would be far on its journey and some time would be necessary for it to overcome its momentum and drop back to Earth even if it did return. Packing up the instruments, we carried them to the car, doffed our cumbersome outfits, and drove away. There was no sense in going back to town, for there was another of the Martian projectiles a few miles distant, and evening was not far off. We dined at a little country inn, and then turned west as the afterglow bathed the world in soft rosy light.

Twilight was fading into night when we reached our destination, and by the time the instruments were set up it was pitch dark. This time we were careful not to get too close to it. To avoid being blown one way and sucked another by the blast of air and the following inrush as the projectile left the Earth, we lay flat upon our faces as Henderson prepared to press the switch. The click of the switch was instantly followed by a rushing roar; there was a strong puff of wind, a breathtaking suction, and the night was lit by a, brilliant green glare. Leaping up, we gazed into the sky. Far above our heads a dazzling ball of greenish fire was sweeping across the heavens. Rapidly it decreased in size; the weird light in which we were bathed faded away, and the speeding, glowing ball became a faint, far-away, luminous speck.

"Now we'll see…" cried Henderson, as he sprang to his instrument, and pressed the switch.

With fast-beating hearts and tensed nerves, we kept our eyes fixed upon that remote speck of light. For an instant it seemed to waver, to remain fixed, and our hearts fell. The next second it flickered and vanished.

"Hurrah!" yelled Henderson. "That's that! Once they get going, there's no coming back. Gosh! I hope a big reception committee's waiting up there to welcome you, old boy—and I hope you smash about ten thousand of 'em."

Then, abandoning his flippant manner, Henderson said most seriously, "It's just as I expected. I've been thinking a lot about it since this afternoon, and I've changed my opinion and ideas some. I've thought all along that the result was produced through an alteration or some effect upon the Martian waves, but I'm beginning to doubt that now. I'm more inclined to think it's in the projectiles themselves, some sort of magnetic property that is shifted from positive to negative by my device so that the things become violently repelled. Or again, it may be gravitational—perhaps when affected by my wave and current they become immune to gravitation and just shoot off into space by centrifugal force."

"I really can't see that it makes much difference as long as they go," I said, "and I don't see how you're going to find out anyway."

"I don't, either," admitted Henderson. "And, as you say, what are the odds? Come, let's see how many we can get going tonight."

"Possibly," remarked Fothergill as we packed up the instruments, "by observing the trajectories followed by the departing objects, we might be able to ascertain which theory is the correct one. If it is the Martian wave that operates them, I should assume that the masses would return to Mars. But if it is merely an anti-gravitational effect, or is due to a reversal of a magnetic property, there is no logical reason why they should return to that particular planet. They would more probably head for the moon."

"Righto!" exclaimed Henderson. "I'll let you try your hand at that, Fothergill. You can keep watch through your telescope tomorrow night, while we shoot the things off. But, personally, I don't care a whoop where they land, as long as they don't land on our old Earth."

HALF an hour later we watched another of the projectiles hurtling like a gigantic blazing cannonball into the sky.

"Gosh almighty!" cried Henderson as it swept upward like a stupendous rocket, and disappeared. "Talk about the Fourth of July! This beats any fire-works display all to pieces!"

When we at last turned toward the city, the eastern sky was paling with approaching dawn, and we had seen four of the Martian projectiles vanish into space.

"I wonder," remarked Henderson with a yawn, "how many people saw the things and what they thought. I'll bet—more than one chap who saw them has jumped upon the water-wagon. And—say, come to think of it, I didn't notice any new ones falling tonight. Did you?"

We shook our heads. "It's strange," I said, "but then, it's not the first night that none has fallen, and besides, some may have fallen on the other side of Earth."

When, towards noon the following day, I reluctantly arose and glanced at the morning paper, I chuckled. "AMAZING PHENOMENA OBSERVED!" I read in glaring headlines. "Incredible as it may seem," began the article, "several of the Martian projectiles, or masses of incandescent material resembling them, were reported last night. This would of course excite no comment were it not for the fact that instead of approaching

Earth, these were moving away from us! Residents of the Catskills declare that they were very brilliant and illuminated the district as brightly as searchlights, but that there were no explosions such as have invariably accompanied the appearances of the projectiles.

"Moreover, the observers declare that they distinctly saw the projectiles rushing upwards and away from Earth and that they gradually dwindled and disappeared. It has long been rumored that moonshining is a thriving industry in the Catskills, and were the reports of departing projectiles confined to the scene of Rip Van Winkle's amazing experiences, we would be inclined to attribute them to the potency of local "mountain dew," But the reports from there are substantiated by innumerable trustworthy and well-known citizens who observed the same phenomena from various widely separated points.

"Inquiry also elicited the fact that at least four of our most eminent astronomers observed the receding projectiles. What does it mean? Are our unwelcome celestial visitors about to retreat and leave us in peace, or is our harassed world ridding itself of its tormentors by some unknown and mysterious power? Undoubtedly Professor Sir Paul Henderson can answer the question, but he is at present absent from the city."

How Henderson will enjoy that I thought as I turned to the other columns. Then the daily forecast caught my eye and I glanced over it. Beneath it, in the space usually devoted to a report of the disasters of the past twenty-four hours, was a brief paragraph that astonished me.

"For the first time Henderson's forecast had not been fulfilled. He had prophesied a fall of the projectiles in southern Europe, and had named Nice, Milan, Venice, Marseilles and Barcelona as the cities liable to suffer. But not one had been hit. A few projectiles had fallen during the preceding day, but without material damage, and not a single one had been reported during the night."

I remembered Henderson's remark about our not having noticed any. What did it mean? Was it merely coincidence that none had fallen after we had hurled the first one into space, or was there some direct connection between that and the sudden cessation of descending projectiles? I was still puzzling over it when Henderson called me.

"Didn't I say we'd have folks guessing?" he chuckled. "But what do you know about the darned things quitting and leaving me flat? If this keeps on, my stock will be down to zero. A prophet who can't prophesy nearer than that is out of luck. All joking aside, though, it's got me guessing. Come on over and let's see what we can make of it."

I found him busy writing an account of his astounding discovery and the night's activities for publication in the afternoon papers.

"No use delaying it," he remarked without looking up from his work. "I've had about a million calls already this morning—all wanting to know what I think about the reports of the things reversing their ordinary procedure, and I've agreed to give my explanation to the press today. There!" He ejaculated in a tone of relief. "*That's* finished. I wonder how the world will take it. But honestly, I can't understand why the blamed things have quit coming. I can't believe it has anything to do with our shooting those five into space—it must be just a coincidence, or perhaps the Martians have exhausted their supply. But it's mighty strange that last night should have been the first night none have fallen in…let's see…nineteen months."

We were still discussing this phase of the matter when Fothergill put in an appearance.

"I think," he announced, "that there is no doubt that the projectile you dispatched returned to Mars. I have been in communication with several astronomers and have secured all possible data as to their observations of the receding projectiles. The sight was sufficiently unusual to attract and concentrate their attentions—and while the data is, I confess, meager, I have worked out the trajectories and am convinced they followed a direct course toward Mars."

"Bully for them!" cried Henderson. "But what's your idea about no new projectiles coming Earthwards last night?"

"That is a matter to which I have already devoted no little thought," replied Fothergill. "Of course I am not very familiar with the science of electricity or the laws of vibratory action. However, speaking from the layman's viewpoint, is it beyond the bounds of possibility that your currents or waves—if powerful enough to repel the masses of Martian matter—might not have so disturbed or affected the Martian waves or apparatus that it became impossible for projectiles to be hurled at us?"

"By gosh, Fothergill, I don't know but that might be the explanation," said Henderson. "No one knows how far vibrations may travel, and no one can state positively whether or not they diminish with distance in space. For all we know, every wave may go vibrating through space forever and reach the most distant stars. And in that case mine may reach Mars and put their sending apparatus out of order. I don't see any scientific reason why—assuming my device reverses the Martian waves or alters them in one place—it shouldn't do the same thing right back where they start. But of course, if it's the other way, if it's an anti-gravitational action or if it's a magnetic effect, it wouldn't work. And it puzzles me how they keep going after I switch off. It doesn't work that way with the pieces in my laboratory; just as soon as I turn off the current, down they come again."

"Isn't it possible," I suggested, "that they only drop back when they are within a certain distance of Earth. But once they get well started, traveling at full speed, their momentum is sufficient to carry them beyond the gravitational pull of Earth and within the attraction of Mars."

Henderson shook his head. "The Lord alone knows," he declared. "But there's one thing certain. If we keep on sending the things off and no more come back, we can feel darned sure we've beaten the Martians at their own game, and that's the one really important thing."

Needless to say, Henderson's announcement of his most astounding and latest discovery not only amazed but elated the entire world. And no one, not even the most pessimistic and skeptical, could question its truth. All knew that projectiles had been seen to shoot into space. He actually had accomplished what he claimed, and it was only a question of time and the installation of apparatus before the last of the deadly things would be sent back to their place of origin.

Henderson had promised that he would demonstrate his discovery again that night and would send several more of the projectiles into the heavens, and tens of thousands of people waited and watched the darkening skies as night approached.

They were not disappointed. Three of the projectiles hurled skyward from the Litchfield Hills that night, their dazzling green light illuminating the country for miles around, and in their flight they were visible to watchers more than two hundred miles distant.

And not a single falling projectile had been reported from any portion of the world since our first successful test of Henderson's apparatus.

Whatever the reason, whatever the explanation, we were convinced (as was the public in general) that the sudden and complete cessation of destructive Martian projectiles was a direct result of Henderson's feat.

The world went mad—delirious with joy. Everywhere there were wild, enthusiastic celebrations and thanksgivings. The world was saved; the Martians were defeated! Once more people could live without fear of being destroyed at any moment. Once again the cities would be safe from sudden and complete destruction.

And nightly, daily, steadily, the great masses of metal from another planet were being projected into space. Thousands of the Henderson repeller devices were being manufactured. Thousands of men equipped with wave-proof outfits were hunting out the fallen projectiles and—by pressing a tiny switch—were hurling the stupendous masses of metal from Earth.

From sundown to sunrise the skies were ablaze with the flaring, speeding, ever-vanishing things. They had fallen to Earth singly, by twos and threes, by dozens. But they were leaving, rushing back to their source, by hundreds, thousands, at a time. Never in the world's history had there been such a wondrous, fascinating, awe-inspiring sight as the countless streaming, fiery objects presented. It was like an incessant display of innumerable skyrockets multiplied ten thousand fold.

No more projectiles fell, no more were seen. The papers ceased publishing Henderson's forecasts. People moved back to abandoned cities. Valuables were replaced in their original resting-places. Within a few weeks nearly all the projectiles lying outside the ruined cities had been disposed of. Only those buried in the ruins they had wrought and those that fell in the most remote districts remained.

Then one day Fothergill burst into the room where I was talking with Henderson. His eyes were wide, his face flushed, his hair rumpled and he was fairly bristling with excitement.

"I've seen it!" he yelled. "It's marvelous, absolutely astounding! There's no doubt about it!"

"Hold on, old man!" cried Henderson. "What's all the shouting about? Talk sense and tell us what it is you've seen. I assume it's something to do with that new telescope of yours. Seen the man in the moon or is old Mars itself coming down to attack us?"

Fothergill mopped his brow and grinned. "Not quite that," he said, more calmly. "But it *does* have to do with the new telescope. I used it last night for the first time—it's the most powerful of its type in the world as you know. And the first celestial object I viewed was Mars. I—"

"Quite natural," commented Henderson. "Well, what *did* you see?"

"It's what I didn't see, that surprised me," declared Fothergill. "I have frequently observed Mars through my own as well as other instruments; I am thoroughly familiar with its various features and I have, of course, been more than usually interested in the planet since you promulgated your theory of the Martian origin of the projectiles. I can state without exaggeration that I am as conversant with the superficial aspects of Mars as with those of Earth itself, perhaps even more so, as I have never had the opportunity of viewing Earth's surface from a distance from which it was observable as a planetary entity. I have, as I have said, devoted a great deal of study to Mars, and it was largely due to my interest in that planet and my desire to see more of its details, that I ordered this new and extremely powerful telescope. In fact—"

"For Heaven's sake, Fothergill, tell us what it's all about!" demanded Henderson. "You certainly didn't get all worked up over anything you've said so far. What was it you *didn't* see. Don't tell me Mars has vanished—that we've smashed it all to pieces by our bombardment."

"No, indeed!" Fothergill exclaimed. "Mars is—or was when I last observed it—still in its accustomed position. But the astonishing thing, the matter that amazed me, is that the face of Mars is completely altered. Several of the larger equatorial canals have completely vanished; others have entirely altered their size and position, and where formerly there were level illuminated areas, there are now shadows indicating irregularities of immense dimensions. In fact, through my superior telescope I could clearly discern the existence of huge craters, quite similar to the lunar craters. There can be but one explanation, Paul. The projectiles hurled back at Mars have created stupendous disturbances upon that planet."

"Three cheers for us!" shouted Henderson, leaping to his feet. "And if I'm not mistaken, the darned things are just beginning to arrive at their destination."

"Jumping Jupiter! What's going to happen on jolly old Mars when they begin to arrive in full force?"

"That I cannot say," declared Fothergill, controlling his excitement with an obvious effort. "But if, as you say, and as calculations indicate, only the vanguard of the projectiles has wrought so much havoc on the planet, I should assume that by the time they have all descended upon its surface, the greater portion of its visible area would be in much the same condition as the battlefields of France during the World War."

Henderson emitted a long whistle. "Good Lord!" he exclaimed. "I hadn't thought of it before, but don't you see, Merritt, and you Fothergill, what will happen up there? Mars isn't anything like the size of Earth, and so the projectiles will be concentrated instead of scattered. Wish we could see 'em landing. Just try to imagine it. Think of hundreds of projectiles, weighing anywhere from one hundred to one thousand tons, banging into poor old Mars in a steady stream! It was bad enough here, but it must be a darned sight worse there."

"You must bear in mind," remarked Fothergill, "that an object that weighs one thousand tons here will not weigh much more than one hundred tons there.

Moreover, the projectiles must of necessity lose a large portion of their weight during their flight through our atmosphere and through that of Mars, due to the frictional heat and the consequent combustion of their gaseous contents."

"Maybe," assented Henderson, "but don't forget they've come the devil of a distance and darned fast. According to the laws of physics, a small body traveling at high speed strikes as hard a blow as a large body traveling at proportionately low speed. And according to your own observations, those things must be banging into Mars with awful jolts."

"I should think," I ventured, "that if they are actually the cause of the Martian surface changes that Fothergill reports, we should be able to see them strike or at least should be able to see their immediate effect should we watch carefully through the telescope."

Fothergill shook his head. "No, even my telescope is not sufficiently powerful for that," he declared. "Although it might be possible to note the changes of the surface as they occur, I am going to communicate with Lick, Harvard, and other observatories and inquire if any unusual changes have been noticed on Mars. I'll communicate with you as soon as I know. And I hope you will both come to my observatory tonight and have a look at the planet."

Within an hour after his departure he called us up.

"I was not mistaken," he announced triumphantly.

"Several astronomers noticed the same disturbances, but they did not associate them with the projectiles. I shall write a monograph upon the subject."

When we entered his palatial home that evening, he was jubilant. And when, after he had adjusted the enormous and complicated telescope that had cost him several fortunes, and I peered into the eyepiece, I did not wonder at his enthusiasm and excitement. There, appearing nearer than the moon shown through an ordinary telescope, was Mars, glowing ruddily, its gleaming ice caps sharp and clear, its surface streaked with the dark lines of its mysterious and puzzling canals.

Even I, unfamiliar with the ordinary aspects of the planet, had no difficulty in seeing the circular and semi-circular shadows that marked immense depressions or craters exactly like those upon the surface of the moon. I noticed, moreover, that several of the canals were broken and interrupted, that several of the craters were in the canals themselves.

I was convinced that Fothergill was right, that the planet was being scarred, blasted, altered; was suffering terrific damage from the projectiles with which the Martians had attempted to destroy Earth.

Henderson, too, was convinced. "It's all up with the Martians," he said, as he gazed into the eyepiece. "Begins to look like the moon already. I've heard some astronomers claim that the craters on the moon were caused by giant meteors, that its atmosphere and possibly even its life forms had been wiped out by meteors in past ages. I wonder if at some time someone—maybe the Martians—tried the same trick on the poor old moon. I shouldn't wonder if by the time we get through, Mars is as dead as the moon is now."

And as the days and weeks passed it began to look as if his words would be borne out. The surface of the planet was speckled with craters; one by one the canals vanished, the ice-caps crept farther and farther from the Martian poles towards the equator, and there were no signs of life, no new canals visible.

Meanwhile the work of ridding our Earth of the few remaining projectiles was proceeding steadily. But it was now slower work. Those that remained were buried in the ruins of the cities and buildings they had destroyed, and vast quantities of debris had to be removed before they could be reached.

In many cases, where they were not deeply buried, they could be projected despite their covering. It was a marvelous sight to see a great pile of broken stone, bricks, masonry and twisted structural steel suddenly erupt like a volcano, to see the stones and beams hurled to every side, and to see a great gleaming, roaring mass burst forth and go screaming upwards into the sky.

But it was dangerous work, the apparatus had to be operated from a distance, and even then one could never feel certain that all of the death-dealing mass had been eliminated. Very frequently the projectiles had been shattered when they struck buildings and other structures; in other cases two or more had fallen side by side, and although one might force its way upward, others of smaller size or more deeply buried might still remain among the ruins. Quite a number of serious accidents and several deaths had already been caused by these conditions during the earlier part of the work. The workmen, thinking they had eliminated the things, removed their wave-proof coverings in order to work more freely, and were struck down by the waves emanating from masses still hidden in the debris.

To obviate all such perils and casualties, and to speed up the reconstructive work, Henderson had invented and was perfecting an improved device of far greater scope and power. This, he explained to me, was to embody both a finder and a repeller. He had discovered, he said, that the so-called death-waves not only affected human and animal tissues—the brain being most susceptible—but that they also affected various inorganic substances. This was particularly true of mineral salts, metallic oxides, blue vitriol, and copper sulfate, which became dull yellow. Copper carbonate changed from green to purple, while gold chloride was transformed from yellow to black. In addition, silver chloride became green and the mercuric oxides became intense blue when acted upon by the waves.

"The trouble is," he declared, "that none of these are affected unless close to within a few inches of the stuff—and the color change is permanent. What I'm looking for is some material that will alter in color when it's a long distance away from a projectile—or even a fragment of a projectile. It must be extremely sensitive to the waves—as sensitive to them as is the human brain—and it must change back to its natural color as soon as it is free from the action of the waves.

"Of course," he continued, "that is not essential, for I can probably restore the normal tint by using my resuscitating waves. If I can find such a salt or oxide, we can then locate a mass of the material, get rid of it, and be sure there are no bits remaining to raise Hades later on. You see, Merritt," he added, speaking very earnestly, "it wouldn't do to have a mite of the damnable stuff hanging about. Even after a city was rebuilt and all had been going on as usual for years, someone might be digging a hole or some kid might be playing in a sand pile and a piece of the stuff would bob up and kill who knows how many people."

"I see your point," I replied. "But I'm afraid you've got a mighty hard job to be absolutely dead certain that not an atom of the stuff remains on Earth. A lot of it must be under water, in ponds, lakes or rivers—and may be dredged or fished up at any time. A lot of it must be in deserts and forests and among mountains where no one suspects it. It's like the dud shells and the floating mines after the World War. Even now they're still turning up at times and causing accidents."

"Yes, but that's different," persisted Henderson. "There is no way of locating those, and no known way of getting rid of them without actually finding them. But with this stuff it's another matter."

"You think so?" I asked.

"Yes," he replied. "If I can locate the things, I can get rid of them even if they're not visible. I admit if they're deep under water they'll probably have to remain there until they decompose and disappear. And of course neither I nor anyone else can cover every square mile of Earth's surface hunting for stray pieces. And you may not have noticed it, but it's darned funny that the stuff goes on sending off those death-waves despite all we've sent back to Mars, and that the chances are ten to nothing that every Martian is dead and gone. Either the things send out the waves of their own accord or else the controlling waves keep on coming from Mars without anyone directing them."

"Yes, I had thought of that," I replied. "But about this new device of yours. Instead of hunting about for the finding material, why don't you make the thing so that you can set it going and be sure that every speck of material within a certain area has been blown into space?"

"Because," he laughed, "there are certain things that are impossible. We can't entirely defy the laws of nature, you know. No matter how powerful my apparatus might be, it couldn't make a five-pound piece of the stuff force its way through a fifty-ton block of granite, a ten ton I-beam, or two or three hundred tons of dust, dirt and broken stone."

"No, I suppose not," I admitted, "but do you think you'll ever find the material you need for your indicator? There are such an unlimited number of salts and oxides, sulfides, chlorides, sulfates, chlorates, carbonates and all, that you could spend years experimenting with them. Even then you might overlook the very one you need. It might be right under your eyes, so obvious that it never occurs to you. It might be any common thing—even common salt. It—"

Henderson gave a yell that startled me and leaped from his chair. "By the Lord, Merritt!" he cried, "that may be the very thing. I'm going to try it."

Now in any story, any fiction, by all the rules of the game, Henderson should have found that salt was the very thing he sought. But this is not fiction and hence it is not surprising that salt was not the desired material. But salt, as everyone knows, is sodium chloride, and once his attention was turned to that metal, Henderson determined to go through the whole known list of sodium salts and compounds.

To do so took some time, but he was amply rewarded in the end. Pure metallic sodium did the trick. It was extremely sensitive to the death-waves and showed marked alteration even beyond the range at which the waves affected the human brain. And the intense ruby red that it assumed when subjected to the waves faded out and disappeared as it was withdrawn from them.

Henderson, of course, was delighted. He insisted that I had succeeded where he had failed but I wouldn't listen to that. I had mentioned salt merely as the commonest thing that came to mind to illustrate my meaning, and salt was a long way from being metallic sodium.

Now that he had the required finder, Henderson very quickly completed his new apparatus. It was very compact and easily portable, and he demonstrated its efficiency in locating the material to Fothergill and myself by a laboratory test. Burying one of his specimens of the stuff under a pile of sand in one end of the room, he placed his apparatus on a movable table at the other end. Telling us to watch the tiny sodium plate in its glass-covered recess, he pushed the table forward. Before he had gone ten feet the plate became pink, it deepened rapidly to red as he advanced, and it was a deep carmine by the time the table was within six feet of the concealed fragment of the Martian projectile.

"I don't know how far away it would detect a large lump," said Henderson, "but I intend to give the whole apparatus a practical test tomorrow. As you know, they haven't finished cleaning up Scranton. They've had a lot of trouble there. They thought they'd gotten rid of the projectile that struck the city, but over a dozen men have been prostrated and two have died. There's a lot more of the stuff hidden in the ruins there somewhere, and I've asked the authorities to let it alone until I could try my new device there. It's a fine chance to test it out. I'd like to have you both come along."

Naturally, both Fothergill and I were interested and glad of the chance, but I had to decline. I had an important engagement that could not be broken and, as it turned out, that engagement unquestionably saved my life.

THE terrible crushing news reached me the next afternoon. Henderson and Fothergill, with several officials and assistants, all equipped with their wave-proof garments, had pushed their way through the tumbled ruins of Scranton's once fine buildings, clambered over piles of shattered masonry, and reached the spot where the projectile had been found. Then Henderson had set up his instruments and all had watched carefully as he moved about, his eyes fixed on the sodium plate. Almost immediately it had indicated the presence of a mass of the material from Mars, and after a short time Henderson had announced that the piece lay buried under the ruins of the armory or very near it. He had declared it was far beyond the reach of the current of the devices previously used and that it was an exceptional opportunity for testing the powers of the new apparatus. Moving a safe distance to one side, gauging this by the color of the plate, he had connected his electrical devices and turned the switch.

No one will ever know exactly what happened. Onlookers, who were watching from a distance, saw a cloud of dust and debris fly into the air. They saw a dark mass, like a huge cannon ball, hurled, screaming into the sky. There was a terrific explosion; stones, timbers, bricks were flung in every direction, and then—silence.

Realizing something was wrong, several brave fellows—not stopping to consider their peril—dashed to the scene to find Henderson, Fothergill, and their companions lying dead among the ruins. Within a few yards of where they had stood was a yawning hole that was found to open into a long-abandoned mine shaft. Whether explosives had been stored in the old shaft and had been ignited, or whether the explosion had been caused by powder or ammunition in the wrecked armory, has never been determined.

But Henderson was dead. Henderson who had saved the world, who had saved mankind, had been sacrificed in the cause of humanity. The entire world was shocked at the terrible news of his death. Every nation went into mourning and rendered every honor to one to whom every individual on Earth owed his life. No man in all the world's history had ever been so widely, deeply, sincerely mourned. Kings, emperors and presidents attended his funeral and walked bareheaded behind his flower-hidden coffin draped with the flags of fifty nations. His loss was irreparable; his untimely death meant more to the world than the destruction of thousands of lives in the terrible crisis that—thanks to him—had now passed, forever.

But Henderson had not sacrificed his life in vain. Strangely enough the device he had been testing when death came to him was uninjured. Others like it were made, and thanks to Henderson's last invention, every vestige of the deadly Martian projectiles was located and hurled back at the planet, that, battered and torn by the very things with which its inhabitants had tried to destroy the world, was soon as dead, cold, and lifeless as the moon itself.

THE END

If you've enjoyed this book, you will not want to miss these terrific titles...

ARMCHAIR SCI-FI & HORROR DOUBLE NOVELS, $12.95 each

D-1 **THE GALAXY RAIDERS** by William P. McGivern
SPACE STATION #1 by Frank Belknap Long

D-2 **THE PROGRAMMED PEOPLE** by Jack Sharkey
SLAVES OF THE CRYSTAL BRAIN by Rog Phillips

D-3 **YOU'RE ALL ALONE** by Fritz Leiber
THE LIQUID MAN by Bernard C. Gilford

D-4 **CITADEL OF THE STAR LORDS** by Edmond Hamilton
VOYAGE TO ETERNITY by Milton Lesser

D-5 **IRON MEN OF VENUS** by Don Wilcox
THE MAN WITH ABSOLUTE MOTION by Noel Loomis

D-6 **WHO SOWS THE WIND...** by Rog Phillips
THE PUZZLE PLANET by Robert A. W. Lowndes

D-7 **PLANET OF DREAD** by Murray Leinster
TWICE UPON A TIME by Charles L. Fontenay

D-8 **THE TERROR OUT OF SPACE** by Dwight V. Swain
QUEST OF THE GOLDEN APE by Paul W. Fairman & Milton Lesser

D-9 **SECRET OF MARRACOTT DEEP** by Henry Slesar
PAWN OF THE BLACK FLEET by Mark Clifton.

D-10 **BEYOND THE RINGS OF SATURN** by Robert Moore Williams
A MAN OBSESSED by Alan E. Nourse

ARMCHAIR SCIENCE FICTION CLASSICS, $12.95 each

C-1 **THE GREEN MAN**
by Harold M. Sherman

C-2 **A TRACE OF MEMORY**
By Keith Laumer

C-3 **INTO PLUTONIAN DEPTHS**
by Stanton A. Coblentz

ARMCHAIR MASTERS OF SCIENCE FICTION SERIES, $16.95 each

M-1 **MASTERS OF SCIENCE FICTION, Vol. One**
Bryce Walton—"Dark of the Moon" and other tales

M-2 **MASTERS OF SCIENCE FICTION, Vol. Two**
Jerome Bixby—"One Way Street" and other tales

If you've enjoyed this book, you will not want to miss these terrific titles...

If you've enjoyed this book, you will not want to miss these terrific titles...

ARMCHAIR SCI-FI & HORROR DOUBLE NOVELS, $12.95 each

D-31 **A HOAX IN TIME** by Keith Laumer
INSIDE EARTH by Poul Anderson

D-32 **TERROR STATION** by Dwight V. Swain
THE WEAPON FROM ETERNITY by Dwight V. Swain

D-33 **THE SHIP FROM INFINITY** by Edmond Hamilton
TAKEOFF by C. M. Kornbluth

D-34 **THE METAL DOOM** by David H. Keller
TWELVE TIMES ZERO by Howard Browne

D-35 **HUNTERS OUT OF SPACE** by Joseph Kelleam
INVASION FROM THE DEEP by Paul W. Fairman,

D-36 **THE BEES OF DEATH** by Robert Moore Williams
A PLAGUE OF PYTHONS by Frederik Pohl

D-37 **THE LORDS OF QUARMALL** by Fritz Leiber and Harry Fischer
BEACON TO ELSEWHERE by James H. Schmitz

D-38 **BEYOND PLUTO** by John S. Campbell
ARTERY OF FIRE by Thomas N. Scortia

D-39 **SPECIAL DELIVERY** by Kris Neville
NO TIME FOR TOFFEE by Charles F. Meyers

D-40 **JUNGLE IN THE SKY** by Milton Lesser
RECALLED TO LIFE by Robert Silverberg

ARMCHAIR SCIENCE FICTION CLASSICS, $12.95 each

C-10 **MARS IS MY DESTINATION**
by Frank Belknap Long

C-11 **SPACE PLAGUE**
by George O. Smith

C-12 **SO SHALL YE REAP**
by Rog Phillips

ARMCHAIR SCI-FI & HORROR GEMS SERIES, $12.95 each

G-3 **SCIENCE FICTION GEMS, Vol. Two**
James Blish and others

G-4 **HORROR GEMS, Vol. Two**
Joseph Payne Brennan and others

www.ingramcontent.com/pod-product-compliance
Lightning Source LLC
Chambersburg PA
CBHW030317180626
46810CB00003B/1123

* 9 7 8 1 6 1 2 8 7 2 1 4 8 *